DEATH AT
DECEPTION BAY

A
Lake
Pines
Mystery

Lake Pines Mystery Series
Murder At First Light
Death At Deception Bay
Murder Of Crows
The Dead Of Winter
The Night Is Darkest
Conspiracy Of Blood

Anna Ledin Thriller Series
The Blackwater Operative
The Phoenix Code
Rogue
Blown

Teen & Young Adult
Unfollowed
Order From Karoo Bridge
Carole And The Secret Queen's Scarf

Genre Fiction
The Hotel Penn
Our Forgotten Year
The Plus One

DEATH AT
DECEPTION BAY

A gripping Lake Pines Mystery

L.L. Abbott

Cover designed by Warren Design

This book is a work of fiction. Names, characters, places, and incidents either are products of the author's imagination or are used fictitiously. Any resemblance to actual persons, living or dead, events, or locales is entirely coincidental.

L.L. Abbott
Visit my website at www.LLAbbott.com

Large Print ISBN: 978-1-989325-46-9

FOR MY BOYS

DEATH AT DECEPTION BAY

When I let go of what I am. I become what I might be.

UNKNOWN AUTHOR

1

October 28, 2015

The air in the room had grown stale, and she squinted against the darkness. Lia couldn't tell how many hours had passed since her attacker grabbed her. Her time spent living on the street, sometimes while high, taught her how to gauge time without a watch or daylight, and she was sure it was close to four days.

She patted the tender spot on her head and felt the dried blood that matted her hair. The heat from the cut behind her ear was a sure sign of an infection and she knew from her three years in the nursing program that it meant she'd need several stitches. The swelling around her wound prevented her skin from healing and she could feel the dampness ooze from the gash. She was losing hope that anyone heard her cries for help on the morning she was grabbed. It was a little before six a.m. and still dark enough to feel like it was the middle of the night, and she had thought was the perfect time to squeeze in a quick run before going to the hospital. The tip of the moon was visible over the line of trees, and the crispness in the air was invigorating.

There was no warning of the attack, nor did Lia see her assailant coming. Lia was half a mile from where she started her run when a sharp blow hit her head from behind. There was no mugging, nor any threat of robbery from her attacker. No matter how hard she tried, she couldn't remember him speaking at all. Anyone could have seen she was in her running gear and, at most, would get her four-year-old portable music device. And if it was the electronics her assailant was after, the extended baseball bat was a tad extreme. Plus, it was still attached to her jacket, and only her earphones were missing.

Lia had stopped digging and clawing at the wooden door, even though it was her only way out of the dark, damp enclosure. Not that she gave up trying to escape but because her fingers had grown raw and cut by her constant ripping at the cold, hard wood. She could feel the uneven edges where her nails snapped back and the nail on the middle finger of her right hand peeled back over the tip of her finger, leaving her fragile skin exposed. Splinters lodged under the tips of her fingers, making it too painful to touch. Lia even resorted to using her hair clip as a tool to remove pieces of the wooden door hoping to carve a hole to the outside, but it had snapped within ten minutes of scrapping against the solid wooden door, and she knew it would be useless.

Lia shivered uncontrollably as she lay curled on the dirt floor, trying her best to stay alive. Her only sign of whether it was night or day, was the small sliver of space between the bottom of the door and the ground that gave way to the traces of light that leaked through. A damp musty scent rose from the ground, and as each evening grew cooler, so did the floor inside her isolated imprisonment. During the first few nights, the chill lay on the surface of the stone walls, but after a while the chilly dampness surrounded her, rooting itself through her body, seeming to pull her deep into the ground. Every night she fought the desire to escape her reality and fall into a deep sleep, worried it would be impossible to awaken from.

She had to stay alert.

It was cooler than normal this fall, and October had seen the beginnings of an early snowfall and Lia wondered just how cold it could get in Lake Pines. She had arrived a week earlier and had planned to move here and begin her nursing career at the Lake Pines Hospital. And if her personal life worked out, then it would even be better. But now all that mattered was escaping from this hell she was living in and getting back to Noah.

Dried blood formed patches on her skin, but she could feel a slow trickle ooze from a few cuts. It was a small sign she was alive and had a chance of surviving if she could make it out of this enclosure and away from the monster that grabbed her. Lia hung onto that hope as she fought against the pain that rose in her body. The one consolation she had was knowing the fierceness at which she fought back against her attacker and how she had removed a chunk of skin from his neck which was left exposed by the small balaclava he wore. It was his scream she remembered hearing before she blacked out, along with the faint scent of patchouli.

She could still feel the bruises where the rocky shoal surface rubbed and tore at her legs as she fought against his grip. Painful stabs along her back pulled her from unconsciousness, when he dragged her across the hard, cold ground and past a large clump of trees, and into the shed where she now lay. That must have been at least three days ago. Maybe more.

The air was hauntingly still and saturated with an unsettling smell. Each breath reminded Lia of the abandoned warehouse she had called home during her two years on the street. It was a stench that you could taste and feel in the pit of your stomach. Those were memories that Lia worked hard to suppress, and they came flooding back with the pervasive scent and had a way of reclaiming the painful recollections.

The muffled sound of singing birds was the only break in the silence that surrounded her enclosure. She didn't know where she was, but she knew it wasn't anywhere that anyone could hear her screams. Lia ran her shaky hand across the surface of the smoothed down stone walls, faintly able to make out an outline of the large rocks at the base. She huddled her body in a corner of the shed, preserving the negligible amount of heat her body still possessed. She crawled over the bare ground, leaving the support of the stone wall, until she reached the wooden door. The distance was short and coated with small rocks. Painful bruises formed on her knees and palms from when she crawled along the ground, assessing the size of her enclosure. Lia knew she must be in an outer building and judging by the restricted space and smell, she thought it was a storage shed.

She spent many hours with her ears pressed against the space along the bottom of the door, hoping for some sound from the outside that could help her determine her location. Not that she could get a message to anyone, she just wanted to know where she was being held and was fighting for her life.

Lia's tears had long since dried and her clothes grew stiff from the mix of the damp ground and her body giving way to the loss of control when she could no longer restrain her bodily functions. She shivered as she drifted in and out of consciousness, trying to hold on to the memory and scent that meant the most to her. When she awoke and kissed Noah good morning, she remembered thinking how perfect her life had seemed as they planned their future together. It took hard work to set things right over the last few years and had made a break from her pattern of poor choices and bad friends. Lia was starting a new life, and now she had someone else to think about. She had a job and a future, and she was trying to do what was right.

She pulled her light blue cotton t-shirt from beneath her running jacket and buried her nose into the material. She inhaled the aroma of soft roses and powder, just like she had done many times over the last few days. It was the one thing that was keeping her focused, and the scent was fading.

She closed her eyes and felt herself slipping into blackness when she heard the snap of the bolt on the outside of the large wooden door, and then it released from the cement frame, bringing with it a blast of the cool night air.

The shadows from the trees outside shaded the entrance to the shed, and along with it, the man who attacked her.

He had returned and still wore the balaclava over his head, shielding his face from his victim and muting the sound of his voice. He came when the night outside was dark and there was little chance of being seen. Lia had tried to make a run for the door the first few times, attempting to catch him off guard. She stopped trying to escape after being kicked in the midsection so hard she felt a rib crack from under the force of his boot. Lia knew even if she managed to make it past him, she no longer had the strength to outrun him. He favored his right arm under the strain on his shoulder and held it close to his side.

He again offered her a choice. One that could see her free to return to her life, if she would stay quiet about what she knew. He threatened to kill her if she didn't agree. But she couldn't. Not after what she had been through. She had seen enough during her time on the streets that she knew he probably wouldn't let her go, anyway. He would be back again with more threats, and the next time it would even be worse. She just needed to buy some time and hopefully, before too long, someone would find her.

However, Lia misjudged her attacker's level of patience and he was no longer willing to wait to change her mind.

Her attacker lifted the balaclava and peeled it away from his face. Even in the dark shed, she could distinguish his features.

Lia looked up and for the first time saw the face of her attacker. She gasped as she lay curled in the corner of the damp cell and cringed as she realized the frightful comprehension of who had attacked her. It was clear now what her assailant wanted. She yelled in protest and finally agreed to his demands, but he shook his head.

"No," he said. "It's too late. I can't trust you."

She slowly lifted her head and pulled her body up to a level where she could rest a little higher against the wall. She took a deep breath and for the first time in three days spoke without tears.

"Why?" she asked.

He didn't answer. He stood over her and coldly stared down at the person he would have done anything to protect. Now she was the one person who stood in the way of his success. He reached into his jacket and pulled out a buck knife. It was the one his father gave him when he was a child and had taken him hunting on his annual fall trips.

"No, please don't," Lia begged.

She wasn't thinking of her wound or the bruises and the cuts that his brutal beating had produced. Lia didn't care if her skin was scarred, or her bones were broken. Her only thoughts were of Noah and how she needed to protect him.

Then all at once, she was consumed by a wave of pain followed by a deep searing heat and became lost in deeper darkness, this one from which she would never return.

2

March 6, 2016

The words from their fight the night before echoed loudly in Kerry's head as she ran along the main road that stretched through the middle of town. The heavy snow from the winter hadn't melted, and the sidewalks had a slippery sheen, and she didn't want to risk falling a second time during her morning run. She learned the hard way the first spring she moved to Lake Pines that living in a town near a large lake meant that damp cold evenings were a reality until late in

June, and she adjusted her clothing and footwear accordingly.

Over the winter, Kerry's old boss from Montreal had been trying to convince her to return to Quebec and head up the coroner's office upon his planned retirement. For the last six months, Doctor Jean Lamont had been calling Kerry with numerous offers hoping to entice her to leave her small practice in Lake Pines and return to Montreal. At first, Kerry laughed at the idea. She had built a quiet, but fulfilling, life in Lake Pines. And even though the cases were not as intense as the ones that she worked on in Montreal, she felt she was able to help families find closure. She had a personal connection with them.

Like most small towns, blurred lines separated the duties between the police investigators and coroner. It was a necessity in Lake Pines which worked under a restrained budget but it also permitted staff to explore other job skills and built a cohesive work environment where things got done. The Province's Minister even went so far as to acknowledge Lake Pines' ability to cover more cases than other small towns their size. And they were often able to do so while staying under budget.

When Kerry took the job as coroner in Lake Pines, she worked closely with Constable Peter George, and together they made a great team. They understood each other's work habits and always held the respect of the victims and their families above their own career goals, and they were able to build a close friendship over the years. However, Kerry was losing interest in her job as coroner in Lake Pines. The small Northwestern Ontario town had lost a fair number of people over the years because of the dwindling economy. Each season another store would shutter their doors and owners who had run successful establishments in Lake Pines decided to close their businesses and retire to their cottage homes, leaving chunks of the small downtown abandoned.

The tight economy even hit the Lake Pines Coroner's Office with cutbacks to her staffing budget. Kerry found the territory she was responsible for had increased even though the support and budget for her office had not. However, it was when Peter moved that Kerry felt a real shift in her career. She had difficulty relating to the policing and management styles of Peter's replacement, Wayne Burgess. He didn't hold Kerry's skill and intuition with the same high regard that Peter did, and more and more Kerry was feeling pushed out of the interesting facets of cases. What frustrated her the most, was that she was still left to answer for the frequent mistakes he made during investigations.

Kerry had also unexpectedly found love in Lake Pines, and for a couple of years, she had been dating Simon Phillips. Simon was a fishing guide from May to October and during the remainder of the year, he ran a winter resort on an island in Deception Bay. Kerry first met Simon at Fox Lodge where Simon was working. The stop on the way to Vancouver was supposed to be a time to rest and rejuvenate while catching up on some much-neglected reading. The day Kerry checked into Fox Lodge a storm had rolled into Northwestern Ontario and cut off all access roads and made the ice road to the lodge inaccessible. Instead of being able to sequester herself by the fireplace in her room, she was huddling in the main room with the two other guests while Simon worked to keep the lodge warm - and the guests fed.

In place of devouring the pile of books she packed, Kerry found herself absorbed in Simon's stories and devouring the wine from the private reserve stock which Simon insisted the owner would want them to enjoy. By the time the roads were cleared, and the storm had passed, Kerry and Simon had realized that they had a lot in common, and she extended her stay. Now, as she was running through the middle of town, Kerry was replaying the argument she and Simon had the night before when she mentioned she was upset about all his side trips out to the cabin over the winter. Simon felt like he had been hit from left field and even accused Kerry of not trusting him. Distrust never existed between them, however, not long after moving in together, Simon spent many weekends away from her at his cabin. Kerry was concerned that the trips were becoming more frequent and that she and Simon were growing apart.

Simon accused her of pushing him away by not trusting him. When in reality, Kerry was hoping their honesty would bring them closer together. Simon explained to Kerry that the trips were important to him because they were a reminder of a time when he and his father shared hunting trips. Every fall they would set out on their annual father-son trip and establish the bond that would last the rest of their lives. Now that his father was gone, it was the one place he felt close to him and he begged her to understand that.

Kerry understood the importance of keeping a memory of Simon's father alive, but what she didn't understand is why most weekends since last fall needed to be spent with Wayne. She was feeling more like an outsider in Simon's life, and with the added difficulty of the restrictions in her job, she was feeling more unhappy every day. The right moment never presented itself, when she felt comfortable mentioning Jean's job offer to Simon. If she was going to decide to move, it would have to be for her own reasons. And she just had to hope that Simon would admit that he wanted to continue their relationship no matter where they lived.

Kerry increased her pace and wiped the tears from her cheeks as she neared the end of Main Street. She turned the corner and could see her office, and her chest tightened. Jean's offer to run the office in Montreal genuinely intrigued her. The idea of having some freedom was the primary draw. Kerry was bright and knew that along with running the coroner's office in Montreal, she could even teach a class at the university, furthering her exposure in the field even more.

Kerry had been running for over half an hour and her dark mood hadn't lifted as she had hoped. Tension mounted, tightening her shoulders, as she recalled the fight she had with Simon. Instead of turning right and heading toward home, Kerry veered off to the left and headed for the trails on Tunnel Island, just outside of town.

The trails were popular with hikers and cross-country skiers, and for that reason, Kerry was sure that the grip along the trail would keep her from slipping. Kerry increased her pace along the fence next to the road and jumped the gate and jogged across the causeway that led into the forested path. Tunnel Island was a popular trail area and accommodated outdoor enthusiasts all year long.

Even during the depths of winter, Kerry could feel the forest full of nature under the towering trees. Some branches clung to the dried leaves of the previous fall, but most had dropped and lay under the slowly melting cover on the ground. The jack pines rose from the rocky ground and stretched over the shore, hanging close to the surface of the water, shading patches on the ground. The scent from the pine trees, even in the frozen winter, filled the air and had a way of clinging to your clothes long after you returned from time spent in the forest.

Birch trees covered most of the island, and at this time of year, the lack of leaves allowed the bright sun to stream across the snow and ice that lay on the forested floor. A mix of boot-trodden snow and ice covered the forest floor, absorbing the dirt below with each stage of thaw and freeze, giving it a glossed-over muddy appearance. Autumn leaves that fell to the ground wriggled through the melting patches of snow, and in about three weeks the complete trail would be muddy and unpleasant for long runs. Especially if the prediction for a rainy spring came to fruition.

Surrounded by the smells of the forest and the silence that the cover of the trees created, Kerry relaxed. Songbirds appeared a week earlier, and Kerry could hear them from their perch as they gathered on the branches of the jack pines. Kerry remembered why she stayed in Lake Pines and how the small Northwestern Ontario town grew on her. It was a refuge for her during a time in her life that she needed to have one, and once she began her job as the town coroner, she also found renewed purpose. But things had changed in both the town and her life and she knew it may also be the right time to make another change.

She decided that she was going to call Jean and accept the job in Montreal, and she would tell Simon that she was going. With or without him. She took a deep breath and increased her pace.

The shimmering patches of ice on the lake were visible through the space between the trees and captivated her. The water lapped at the shore from underneath the breaks in the jagged edge of ice that stubbornly clung to the rocks, echoing each wave through the forest. Kerry took a deep breath of the crisp morning air when she was suddenly pulled to the ground.

Her right foot should have landed flat on the path. Instead, the tip of her toe caught a root and sent her body twisting through the air. She landed with a thud and rolled over on her right shoulder and into a ditch that ran alongside a large fallen tree. Kerry moaned at the pain that shot through her shoulder and knee. She cursed at her inattentiveness on the trail and the stupidity of her fall. She landed face down in a mix of snow and gravel when she came to rest by the enormous log. Kerry spit out the frozen contents of the ground and pushed herself onto her knees. She placed her hand on the side of the fallen tree trunk and used it to support the weight of her body as she pulled herself to her feet.

She sat on the log and brushed the front of her jacket, now torn by her fall, and rubbed her knee. She stood and arched her back and limped toward the path where she tripped.

Kerry reached down and grabbed the root, and gave a powerful tug. It came loose in her hand and sent her stumbling backward, almost falling into the ditch from where she just crawled out from.

Kerry stared at the path and then looked down at her hand. Instead of a root, Kerry was holding a ripped piece of clothing and from the ragged ground peered the frozen foot on which Kerry had just tripped.

Unfazed by the sudden appearance of a dead body, Kerry calmly removed her phone from her pocket and dialed the number for Constable Wayne Burgess. And for now, Simon, Montreal, and her run would have to wait.

3

Constable Wayne Burgess arrived just how Kerry had assumed he would, and exactly like he was trained not to approach a crime scene. When she had called Wayne, she described the scene in the forest and told him an ambulance wasn't necessary. Except for her footsteps approaching the area, there didn't seem to be any other tracks and she hoped the area hadn't been disturbed. Kerry cursed herself for tugging at the victim's sock. Crime scenes could be fragile, and even though the tip of the victim's foot was exposed it could still hold microscopic traces of evidence. Kerry jogged in place to try and keep warm and when she heard the sirens approaching from a distance, she stopped jogging and rolled her eyes. She didn't think she would have to explain that sirens weren't necessary, but she was proven wrong.

"Damn it, Wayne," Kerry mumbled, knowing he was prone to flipping the siren at any opportunity. It was Wayne Burgess' way of letting everyone know he was the lead constable in town and that he was 'on the scene'. Kerry knew Wayne was trying to live up to Peter's high standards and reputation, but there was no way Wayne Burgess was ever going to replace Constable Peter George.

Kerry waited and watched as Wayne and three junior constables made their way along the path toward where she was waiting near the body.

"Woah, stop there!" Kerry held up her hand with her palm facing the four approaching officers. "We don't know how much of this area needs to be exhumed. We may not have a significant chance of finding any evidence, but we don't want to take any chances."

Kerry could see from where she stood six feet away that the blush of embarrassment rose in Wayne's cheeks. "That's right, crew. Just like I said. Stand back and let me investigate first." Wayne motioned for the three other officers to stand behind a fallen tree and wait for further instructions. He stepped gingerly around the area on the ground where he saw the victim's foot protruding.

"The victim is already dead, Wayne," Kerry said. "You don't need to tiptoe around the body."

Kerry used a tone that mimicked wit to deal with the frustration she felt in working with Wayne. She didn't see any reason to hurt his feelings, and she learned when she first worked with him he didn't welcome advice. That added to the fact that he and Simon were lifelong friends didn't help their working relationship. For Simon's sake, she tried to be patient with Wayne.

"Ha, hilarious Doctor Dearborne. I just don't want to slip," Wayne explained as he made his way across the frozen ground.

He made his way around the body and stood beside Kerry, where he got a look at her torn coat and dirt smear from her fall.

"Are you okay?" Wayne pointed to Kerry's jacket.

"Yeah. I took a spill over the victim's foot. That's how I found the body," Kerry explained.

Wayne placed his hands on his hips and stared down at the body. "I'm surprised that no one came across the body until now."

Kerry nodded, "There's been a lot of snow this year, and it was probably completely covered the entire winter."

Wayne clapped his hands together and looked up at the three junior officers, who were still waiting for their orders from ten feet away.

"Okay, guys. Let's get the area cordoned off and let's keep anyone from stumbling upon the path." Wayne then turned to Kerry. "I'll get the proper crew out here to exhume the body. Do you want to be present?"

"I may as well since I'm already here." Kerry didn't want to leave Wayne alone and in charge of the frozen remains, so she agreed to stick around.

Unlike Peter, Wayne didn't want Kerry working on crime scenes. He said it may cause some concern if they ever had to defend any of their findings in court. Although Kerry wasn't a forensic anthropologist, she had a solid track record, and she proved she could do the job well. Lake Pines could barely afford their own coroner and full police department. However, because of provincial regulations, they had both. Waiting for qualified staff to drive in from nearby towns was more of a detriment to the cases than having Kerry working on them.

The cold from her morning run was settling uncomfortably into her body as her sweat cooled and froze in the layers of her clothes. Kerry shivered and pulled her arms close to her body as she pulled out her phone.

Kerry held her breath as the number rang four times, and then Simon answered on the fifth. She wasn't sure if he'd answer after their argument the night before, but when she heard his voice, it reminded her that he was not the kind of person to hold a grudge.

"Hey Kerry, how was your run?" Simon said over the faint hum of his truck in the background.

"Good, I guess. I need a favor. I am out on Tunnel Island and, well, I stumbled over a body. Literally. I need to stick around so I can make sure the body is removed properly and all the evidence is secured and not tainted."

"You're kidding, right?" Simon asked.

"No, unfortunately, I'm not." Kerry shoved her shivering hand into her pocket.

"Ah, let me guess. The siren I heard was Wayne charging to the rescue." Simon laughed at the other end of the phone and Kerry felt a pang of guilt for making a rash decision to leave Lake Pines for Montreal.

Kerry turned her body away from Wayne as he busied himself giving orders to the other three officers. He was securing police tape around a barrier of trees circling the body, and he seemed to be doing that without fault.

"Exactly. I am going to be here a while and need a warmer coat. Could you -,"

"On my way," Simon answered before Kerry had even finished asking the question.

"I'll wait by the police cars next to the entrance to the path," Kerry said.

"I'll be there in ten minutes," Simon said. Then before he ended the call, he added, "It's a good thing Lake Pines has such a dedicated coroner."

Kerry slipped her phone back into her pocket and for a moment contemplated calling Jean in Montreal and asking him for some time to finish this case before giving him a decision.

She walked along the path she ran on earlier and made her way out to the street where the flashing lights of the police cars were still flickering. A rotating mix of blue and red from the emergency lights reflected off the bare forest trees. Passing cars slowed to catch a glimpse of the cause of the commotion, and maybe to gather some information they could share in town.

Yes, Kerry thought. Death is different in a small town, but the importance of finding justice was the same.

4

It was late afternoon by the time the victim's body was exhumed and brought to Kerry's office in the middle of town. Each item of clothing was placed into separate evidence bags, with a special note made for the sock she inadvertently removed from the victim's foot. The lack of decomposition made determining the cause of death easier, and the wounds on the young woman's body easier to examine. It was clear the victim's body remained frozen from the moment she was buried. In fact, the body still felt the chill from the frozen ground from where it was removed just earlier that day.

Important clues from organs and tissues would be essential in determining the victim's whereabouts in the hours and days before she died. Kerry wanted to work quickly in hopes that it could help give a name to the woman laying on the table in front of her.

As Wayne shouted instructions to the crew tasked with removing the body, Kerry watched every step. The skills of the other personnel on the scene didn't concern her. She had worked alongside them since she first arrived, and she had faith in their competence. It was Wayne's attention to detail that was lacking.

Kerry worked alone for the last year and a half after the wave of cutbacks hit her office. A small town didn't warrant the staff of students or associates looking to be trained. Kerry enjoyed the students when the budget allowed her to take them on as staff since it also satisfied her interest in teaching. However, Kerry also learned to appreciate the quiet, even though she felt that she had lost something from not having students around to guide. Jean's offer in Montreal was so appealing because it could mean that Kerry could also teach at the university from time to time.

Kerry refocused her attention on the victim who lay stretched out on the stainless-steel table in the middle of her examination room. She kept the room at sixty-eight degrees and since she was still feeling the chill from the run earlier, she slipped on a second lab coat to keep her hands from shivering.

The young woman had no visible tattoos or scars and she was either in her late twenties or early thirties. Kerry shuddered as she documented the clothing the victim was wearing. It was a process that Kerry followed every time a body came through her office, but she couldn't help by being shaken because the victim was wearing a similar outfit to the one Kerry had on when she tripped over the body. The girl didn't have any identification on her, which was not uncommon for anyone who was out for a quick jog. Except for her phone, Kerry didn't carry any identification when she left the house that morning. She thought maybe she should change that.

Even with the damage done when the body was buried in the forest on Tunnel Island, Kerry could see that the girl had sustained a horrible beating before she died. Her head showed signs of trauma, however, due to the amount of swelling around the wound, Kerry estimated that the victim was hit several days before she died. The damage to her skull also indicated that it was probably not the cause of death. There were numerous scrapes to the victim's body, some postmortem, from when she had been dragged along the ground. Blood and dirt stained the victim's fingertips and several of her nails had broken off in an uneven and jagged shape. Kerry positioned the magnifying glass over her hand and inspected each finger. Small slivers of wood had splintered and lodged themselves under her skin, and one nail was almost ripped from the tip of her finger. A small amount of skin tissue was embedded under the nails on the victim's right hand, the only trace of her attacker. After removing the wood slivers and samples of skin, they were placed in sterile containers and labeled for the lab technician who would be conducting the tests. Kerry continued to search the body for other signs that could point to where the victim had spent the last few days of her life.

Along with the large gash behind the victim's ear, Kerry noticed a minor cut and impression on the top of her head. Kerry knew from the many times she banged her head against the cupboards in the kitchen that the markings were most likely caused by a hair clip being struck against her skin. However, there was no hair clip among the victim's belongings.

Both victim's shoes were missing, and the running jacket had numerous rips along the seams. One tear held Kerry's attention. It was at the midpoint of a large blood soak that saturated the front right side of the victim's jacket and Kerry surmised it was the final cause of death. But a full autopsy would confirm it. Kerry measured the slit at less than a tenth of an inch thick and about two and a half inches long and made her think it was most likely a hunting knife. Being stationed in a small town meant that there were many hunting and fishing enthusiasts, and along with them came the common tools of the trade which Kerry learned to recognize.

She carefully removed the victim's clothing and searched the pockets for remnants of receipts that might identify where the victim had been before her death. The clothes were not from specialty clothing stores and were well-worn. She let out a frustrated sigh, knowing there was little chance of tracing where the victim may have purchased them.

Kerry worked for the next four hours tagging and recording each piece of clothing, and she began her autopsy.

Many of her friends wondered how someone so outgoing and jovial could enjoy her job as a coroner. Kerry said that it was for that reason that she enjoyed her friends when she did see them. She learned to appreciate life in her attempt to give closure to the many lives cut short. Simon never questioned her choice of career nor did he ask her the specifics about any of her cases, which she appreciated. He always could sense when she had a particularly tough day, and was at the ready with a glass of wine and a hot bath.

Pushing thoughts of Simon and their future out of her head, Kerry continued to prep the body for a full autopsy.

Kerry scribbled notes that to some would seem irrelevant, but she found when they were viewed alongside other clues that they could give an identity to the victim or the killer. '*No clue is too small*' Jean had told her on her first day, and Kerry never forgot that.

When she finished the autopsy, Kerry prepared the body for storage. She always hated that term 'prepped for storage'. It seemed so cold and distant. It was important for Kerry to make sure that the victim's family had closure and to do that she wanted to make sure there was no further or unnecessary trauma to the body. Photographs of the victim were uploaded to her computer and she forwarded a copy to Wayne.

Kerry peeled off her gloves and rushed out of the chilly examination room. She turned up the thermostat and poured a hot coffee before beginning her paperwork.

She was no longer shaking, but neither was she warm. Kerry turned on her computer and began to fill in the information she collected into the Victim Identity Form. She hated looking at the top of the form and seeing an alphanumeric code in the spot that the victim's name should be.

Some of the key things Kerry discovered on the victim were standard. Three fillings in her teeth, her wisdom teeth had been removed, and she had a slight tear in her right shoulder blade muscle that had healed and scarred from the damage many years earlier. The victim's left ear showed signs of a recent infection, but the blood tests would determine if she was on any antibiotics. Kerry also extracted a small black fiber from the victim's inner ear and bagged it for testing.

When it came to murder cases, Kerry would add information she thought specifically could help the police lead their investigation to the killer. And as this victim was obviously murdered, Kerry began to type in the few pieces of information she felt could help capture the killer. One. Judging by the location of the wound, the killer was most likely left-handed. Two. The murder weapon was some sort of hunting knife. Three. It was also a possibility that the killer was not strong enough to carry the victim since it looked like she was dragged along the ground. Kerry also made a note that the skin found under the victim's nails would also hold the DNA for the killer. However, they would have to wait for those results to come back.

Kerry was able to draw four vials of blood from the victim along with tissue cultures. She then decided to get the fifth sample of blood to add to the test batch. She also collected samples of fluids from the victim that could give her clues to what she ate or even where she may have been. The victim's lungs may also still hold particles that could indicate where she had been in the days leading up to her death. The contents of her stomach were empty which means it was a good guess that she was out for a run in the morning before she had a chance to grab breakfast or a day's worth of food.

But what concerned Kerry was what she had found during the last part of the examination. The victim had a horizontal scar across the lower part of her pelvis. It was clear that the victim had delivered a child by cesarean, and what troubled Kerry is that judging by the internal healing and outer marks on the skin, the procedure was close to only a year old. But not much longer. There was a baby out there who was missing its mother.

As Kerry typed the last entry into her file, she vowed to replace the alphanumeric code at the top of the sheet with a name. She owed the victim's baby that much.

5

The museum fundraiser was not where Kerry wanted to spend her evening, but she knew that Simon was counting on her to be there since he was part of the six-person planning committee that worked to get it renovated. Being a resident of such a small town, it was hard to avoid functions that were important to Lake Pines. Although Kerry tried to think of an excuse, she couldn't come up with one that would excuse her absence, and in the end, she knew it wouldn't be worth the grief.

Local craft makers and artisans displayed their goods across wooden tables that were set up in the middle of the room. Shop owners and private artisans took full advantage of any event that guaranteed a gathering of many of the people from Lake Pines, hoping to garner a few extra sales. Guilt was often the driving force behind most purchases. It was easy to walk past a small shop on Main Street but it was considerably more difficult to explain to Mrs. Thorne why you didn't need a third hand-painted birdhouse in your backyard.

"I think this little blue one would complement your lawn furniture out back," Mrs. Thorne held the small wooden birdhouse in her slim hand. The skin on her boney fingers was transparent and covered in light brown spots that formed over her time in the sun. Like most of Mrs. Thorne's customers that evening, Kerry pulled a twenty-dollar bill from her pocket and handed it over in exchange for the birdhouse.

"I don't have any change, dear," Mrs. Thorne said while gripping the twenty-dollar bill in her hand. Kerry, like Mrs. Thorne's previous customers, told her to keep the change.

Along with not arguing about the price, Kerry followed suit with the other new owners of Mrs. Thorne's birdhouses and declined to point out that each birdhouse was identical except for a slightly different color in paint. At ninety-two Kerry figured she achieved the right to a few leniencies in her sales tactics and methods.

Kerry moved along the other tables where artisans were selling a collection of items and respectfully glanced at the objects they had laid out. There were handmade pieces of jewelry, knitted sweaters along with soaps and candles. Kerry was not in the mood for shopping and thankfully the other sellers were not as forceful as Mrs. Thorne.

Kerry accepted the second glass of wine as she walked around the museum halls and glanced at the local artist's paintings and read the plaques that were affixed beneath them. She especially was fond of Kate Quarry's watercolor paintings. She captured the rawness of the Northwestern Ontario region while expressing the softness of its residents. Kerry purchased one of Kate's paintings the first year she arrived and when Kate was an up-and-coming artist. That was a few years ago, and Kate was no longer a starving artist.

The latest painting was titled 'Abandoned'. It was a scene of a long–forgotten island somewhere on Lake Pines. The dilapidated building was falling into itself and looked like it had not welcomed visitors in decades. The steely gray sky was streaked with clouds from a storm that had just passed over the area. Trees and brush were flattened by the passing storm and lay strewn over the rocky shoal shoreline. Waves pounded against the rocks and the brushstrokes captured sprays of dark water as they shot into the air. The feeling was sad. Memories of a once-loved place were forgotten over time and battered by life. However, Kerry found herself strangely attracted to it.

"Doesn't Kate just capture the essence of Lake Pines?" the voice came from Bernard Wessex, the mayor of Lake Pines.

Bernard first ran for office when he was twenty-two and fresh out of college. It was the year that everyone on the city council was nearing retirement and every seat was up for grabs. Bernard, not knowing what to do for a career, threw his hat in the ring on a bit of a lark. After a night of drinking, it didn't take much convincing when three of his friends challenged him to run for office. Or so that is how Simon told the story. And after meeting Bernard it was easy to believe that's exactly how he found his way into politics.

Bernard easily won his seat as mayor since no one else ran for the position. As was the case for the other council positions that needed to be filled that year. Eventually, each seat was filled, and the small-town council was established. As the mayor, Bernard was involved in every fundraising and cultural event in Lake Pines. When Bernard first won his seat, the economy was on a major downturn and he had difficulty obtaining the funding for essential services in the town. Somehow Bernard managed to use the skills and training he received at college as a wildlife engineer and secured government funding for the region surrounding the town. This allowed Lake Pines to create jobs that would service the outlying forested areas and they created protected park areas that could be used for both recreation and education.

Because of Bernard's ability to secure connections and contacts with government personnel, jobs were created and businesses were established as an offshoot to the tourist traffic that steadily came through Lake Pines. The residents were pleased with Bernard's track record of job creation and he has been re-elected ever since. No one ever asking a single question of how he was able to do any of what he did.

"Shame about the girl that was found though," Bernard whispered to Kerry.

"Yes, very much so," she answered. Kerry didn't like to talk about her cases outside of official capacity, and especially where the citizens of Lake Pines could overhear any details.

"I was hoping we can keep this quiet for now," Bernard suggested in a whisper. "We don't want to alarm any citizens or tourists with this."

"A girl was murdered Bernard," Kerry snapped, but only loud enough for Bernard to hear.

"Oh, I understand Kerry. It's just that with this museum getting off the ground and Lake Pines trying to raise tourist numbers it could scare off some new businesses I am trying to attract to the area," Bernard explained, hoping he didn't sound too insensitive.

Kerry let out a deep breath, "I'm sorry Bernard. I just want to make sure that the victim gets some justice in all of this."

"And that's why Lake Pines is so lucky to have such a dedicated coroner on staff," Bernard returned his attention to the painting.

"I was thinking that Kate should design the new town sign that we'll be putting up on the highway this summer. What do you think Kerry?" Bernard asked.

"I didn't know a new sign was going up," Kerry said, pleased that the topic had changed.

"I think it's about time to freshen things up around here," Bernard looked past Kerry and caught sight of Abigail Irvin on the other side of the room and threw his hand in the air, and waved in her direction. Bernard had been asking Abigail out for a date over the last year and a half and although she never agreed to go out with him, she didn't turn him down either. That was enough to keep Bernard on the line and his hopes in the air. What Bernard didn't know was that Abigail had two other men in Lake Pines vying for her attention and had kept them hanging on as well.

Jim Chandler walked into the museum and motioned to Kerry from across the room. He grabbed a drink from the hostess and began to walk around the museum greeting the many people in the room that were not only his customers but his friends as well.

Bernard wrinkled the napkin in his fist and started to walk toward Abigail Irvin on the other side of the room, "Excuse me, Kerry."

And in a flash, Bernard was off.

Kerry was left alone for a few moments before Simon came up and stood beside her.

"Here, I brought you some food," Simon handed Kerry a small plate with a variety of appetizers. "I assumed you probably didn't eat much today. Especially after finding the body this morning. How is that going?"

"Okay. Thanks for asking. I just hope Wayne doesn't screw things up on this," Kerry said.

"You need to give Wayne a chance Kerry. He's not a bad guy, he just needs a little while longer," Simon said.

"I know you are friends Simon, but it is very different when you have to work with him," Kerry explained.

"I think it has more to do with you wanting to work with Peter again," Simon said.

Kerry shot Simon a surprised look, "I'm capable of keeping my opinion of Wayne separate from my respect for Peter. Just because I preferred working with Peter doesn't mean I haven't given Wayne a fair shot."

Simon held up his hand in defense, "Sorry, just my opinion."

Kerry continued to defend her comment, "I know you have been friends with Wayne since, well, forever. But he's constantly screwing up evidence, he has no tact when approaching families and never thinks before he opens his mouth. It is getting harder to work with him."

Kerry was just about to bring up the job offer she received from Jean in Montreal when Simon began to speak first.

"Kerry, I think you are getting too involved in your cases. You seem too emotional over them," Simon said.

"Emotional? Simon, a person has been murdered. A young girl. And since when have you been so interested in my cases?"

"Since you have been withdrawn and distant from me," Simon said.

"I need to just see this one through," Kerry took a sip of wine and turned away from Simon's gaze, and stared at the painting that was hanging on the wall in front of her.

"Well, then maybe you need to do this without me here," Simon's terse reply took her by surprise. "I'm going to go out of town for a bit. To clear my head."

Simon put his glass on a table and pulled his keys from his pocket, "Good luck with your case Kerry. I'll call you when I get back and we can talk then."

Simon turned away from Kerry and walked toward the exit and pushed open the door to the front lobby and walked out.

Kerry was left standing in front of Kate's painting, holding back the tears that were threatening to burst. As she stared at the scene of the rocky shoreline, absent of trees and people, Kerry, like the aptly-named painting felt alone and abandoned.

6

Simon pushed through the crowd of people standing around the raffle table dropping their five-dollar tickets into bags that would be shaken later and a prize chosen for the winners. Volunteers busied themselves as they swarmed guests from the moment they walked in the doors until the time they freed twenty dollars from their wallets for a strip of green tickets. Although there wasn't a shortage of prizes donated by the businesses in Lake Pines, there was a lack of interest in winning them, and raffle tickets were purchased out of a blend of guilt and support for the museum. Simon tossed sixty dollars' worth of tickets into the bag that was designated for Jim's marina as he headed toward the door. The winner would receive a full year of docking and it was the only prize Simon could see worth winning. It was also the only bag that was stuffed full of tickets. The second most popular prize was for a bag of coffee beans and four cups that Lisa had donated from her café, Joe Blacks. Simon plucked one of the raffle tickets from Jim's marina prize bag and dropped it into the one from the café. That he could see using.

Simon reached the exit without catching Jim pulling him back inside for another drink. All he wanted to do now was to get as far away from the museum and Kerry, as fast as possible. He didn't know how things had become so tense between them and he struggled to find a way to fix it. With everything that happened last fall, Simon just wanted to get to a point where there was some peace in his life. And he hoped that included a future with Kerry. Simon just wished that she wasn't working on this case. Things between her and Wayne were already tense and awkward, and this case was bound to blow things up between them for good. And Simon was going to be caught in the middle.

He reached his truck which was parked next to Kerry's Jeep, unlocked the door, and climbed inside. He didn't hesitate or look behind when he turned the engine on and put the truck in reverse, narrowly missing Mrs. Johnson who was driving in behind him. After a short wave, Simon peeled out of the parking spot and headed down the road that led out of town.

He was too upset to think about going home and he had no intention of returning to the museum fundraiser, no matter how much he knew Bernard would pressure him about it tomorrow.

Without planning about where he was going, Simon headed down to the marina and where his boat was docked. He parked his truck in the rear of the building, which was reserved for the marina staff, and where Jim always allowed him to park. Simon grabbed his coat and stepped over the low fence next to the lot and made his way down to his boat.

Within a few minutes, he was on his way out of the bay and traveling toward Fox Lodge. He hadn't been out to the lodge since last fall and he needed to get out there and clean up any evidence that he was there with Wayne. With the spring thaw underway, he was able to travel a path of open water the entire distance to Deception Bay. And with the strong current in the area, the ice was sure to be gone and he would have easy access to the dock on the island. And he knew it would be one of the last times he could make it out there without being seen.

7

Kerry shook the aspirin bottle and the last two tablets rolled into the palm of her hand. She tossed them in her mouth and gulped a full glass of water. The hot stream of water loosened her tense neck muscles but had failed to shake the headache that woke her up. Simon hadn't called nor did he return any of her texts. He probably went to his cabin, which is where he had been disappearing to a lot over the last year. Especially when he needed some quiet. But he never needed to go there to get away from Kerry when they first started dating. Maybe it was time for her to think about leaving Lake Pines. Maybe it was the perfect opportunity to take a position in Montreal with Jean.

Kerry pulled her thick knit turtleneck over her damp hair and wiggled her arms into the sleeves. She would miss the relaxed dress code if she were to leave her job in Lake Pines, but that wasn't reason enough to stay.

Thunder rumbled outside and the melodic tapping of rain on the roof filled her head. Kerry loved the rain, especially on the lake. The sound of the distant thunder, high above her, bore the telltale signs that the storm was going to sit over the region for several days. Kerry slipped into her jeans and made her way downstairs where she drifted toward the smell of the fresh coffee that had just finished brewing.

Simon bought Kerry the automatic coffee brewer their first Christmas together. The high-end unit ground the beans in the same carafe that brewed them for a fresh pot of coffee every morning. It was an extravagant gift, and one that Simon saw no need for himself, however, he knew it was something that Kerry would love and drove all the way to Winnipeg to buy it for her.

The thunder continued to rumble as Kerry popped two slices of bread into the toaster and heated the pan on the stove. Her phone buzzed, just as she cracked two eggs into the sizzling pan.

Thinking it was Simon calling, Kerry dashed to answer the call before she looked at the screen.

"Simon?" Kerry answered the phone.

"Sorry Kerry, it's me, Wayne," Wayne Burgess never called her outside of office hours, and rarely by her first name. She wasn't even sure if she had his personal number in her phone. "Is it a good time to talk?"

"Yeah Wayne. I am just making some breakfast. What's up?" Kerry asked.

"I read your report on the victim. Sad business, her having a kid and all," Wayne said. "I decided to put out an alert and I gathered a list of babies born in the last twelve months in the town as well as surrounding areas."

Kerry knew that she had suggested it in her report but decided to let Wayne think it was his idea.

"Did you find anything?" Kerry asked.

"I only received a shortlist. There was only one mother who matched the general description of our victim. I traced it to a hospital in Thunder Bay. There was a young girl who gave birth at the hospital there and she put her baby up for adoption," Wayne explained.

"How long ago was the baby born?" Kerry asked.

"Ten and a half months ago," Wayne said.

"Sounds about right judging by how far her incision had healed. What is the girl's name," Kerry grabbed a pen and paper and was ready to write down the contact information.

"That's the thing, Kerry, the hospital said the girl left without giving them her real name. She just told the nurse she wanted to give the baby up for adoption.

The nurse went to get her supervisor and a social worker and by the time they returned they said the girl was gone."

"Damn it," Kerry cursed at the same time as the sky burst with another series of rumbling.

"I can drop the list off at your office for you if you would like Kerry," Wayne offered.

"No, don't bother. Thanks, Wayne," Kerry disconnected the call before Wayne could respond.

The toaster popped, pushing her warmed bread up and Kerry turned toward the sound. Smoke drifted from the pan, her eggs now black around the edges. She dropped the pan under a stream of cold water, dousing the smoke, and sending a plume of steam toward the ceiling.

Breakfast would be the two slices from the toaster and after she filled her travel mug with coffee, she slipped into her raincoat and dashed for her car which was parked on the street in front of her house.

Kerry's office was only a few minutes from her home and Wayne's office was directly in between the two. At the last second, Kerry decided to stop off and get the list from Wayne and see if he had missed something. It wouldn't be the first time he missed an important detail.

Kerry parked and then pulled the hood on her raincoat over her head. The thunder echoed in her Jeep and the rain danced on her roof. When she cut the car's engine the wipers stopped, and the rain blurred her view from her windshield. She was going to get soaked.

Kerry released the handle and pushed open the Jeep door and made a dash for the police building across the street. By the time she reached the front door, the heavy rain drenched the bottom half of her pants.

Once inside the building, she shook the loose water from her coat and pulled back her hood.

"Kerry, I could've come to your office," Wayne was standing at the door pulling his coat closed as he was making his way out the door.

"That's okay Wayne. I changed my mind on my way to work. I will get a copy of that list if you don't mind."

Wayne paused for a moment and then turned around and headed back into the station and walked toward his desk. He reached up to pull the door open and jerked back his right arm in pain.

Kerry lunged forward and grabbed the door before it hit Wayne in the shoulder, "What is wrong with your arm?"

"I hurt it loading up some supplies for the cottage last fall and it seems to flare up when the weather gets damp. I was just heading out to get a head start on some fishing this weekend but come on in and I'll get that sheet for you.

Kerry held the door open for Wayne and followed him to his desk. Paper and files cluttered the top of his desk making, Kerry closed her eyes and shook her head, "Wayne, how can you keep track of anything here?"

Wayne blushed and without raising his face toward Kerry's gaze he pushed around the papers on his desk until he found the sheet he was looking for, "Here it is!" He handed the printout with the information he compiled from the surrounding hospitals. It included the mother's names, dates, and even the names of the doctors who delivered the babies.

"As I said on the phone, the only mother who matched a description of our victim was the mother who gave birth at the hospital in Thunder Bay about ten months ago, but there's no name for her," Wayne explained.

"Is it okay if I copy this?" Kerry asked.

"Sure, I'll get Officer Jones to get that done for you," Wayne waved Officer Clayton Jones over to his desk. He sprang up from behind his desk and walked over to where Kerry and Wayne were standing.

"Yes sir," Clayton said.

"Can you get Doctor Dearborne a copy of the list of mothers and hospital information we collected this morning? I have to head out right now."

"Sure thing boss," Officer Jones took the sheet and headed to the photocopy machine and placed the sheet on the glass.

Wayne thanked Kerry and said he'd call when he returned after the weekend.

Officer Jones grabbed the sheet from the photocopier machine and looked at it perplexingly.

"What's the problem? Is it out of ink?" Kerry asked.

"No Doctor. It just doesn't seem to be the right list, well not all of it anyway," Officer Jones lifted the sheet in the air.

"I don't understand," Kerry said.

Officer Jones went to his desk and from a neatly organized folder, he extracted a printed sheet like the one Wayne had in the haphazard pile on his desk.

"This is the sheet I gave to Constable Burgess this morning," He held out the sheet so Kerry could read it.

Kerry saw right away what Officer Jones was referring to. The mother that Wayne said gave her baby up for adoption did in fact have a name. And an address as well. Kerry couldn't understand why Wayne altered the list and she sure wasn't going to ask his junior officer.

"Can I hang onto your copy?" Kerry asked.

"Of course, Doctor Dearborne," Officer Jones said.

Kerry folded the sheet and slipped it, along with Wayne's altered list, into her coat pocket to keep them from getting wet as she made her way back to her car.

Kerry thanked the young officer once more and then pushed open the door to leave. With one hand on the door, Kerry turned around, "Oh, and can we keep this between us. Just for now."

"Of course," and the young officer made the motion of locking his lips with a key.

Kerry smiled and pulled her hood over her head. And as she dashed across the street to her Jeep, she thought that maybe she had finally found someone she could work with at the police department. At least for this last case.

8

Kerry hung up the phone in frustration after half an hour of trying to track down the nurse who was working the night the baby was born in the hospital in Thunder Bay. She had retired three months ago, and the current staff was reluctant to release any information over the phone, no matter who was calling. Kerry opened her email and began to send a formal request to the hospital administrator and detailed not only the information she required by the reason why. She hoped that the idea of a deceased mother would be enough to tug at the heartstrings of any bureaucrat.

Once Kerry had sent the email, her alert flashed up on her screen. The lab had the report back on the slivers of wood that were found under the victim's fingernails and skin. Kerry read past the formal legal ease that preceded the findings and had to reverse her eyes and re-read the crucial text a second time. They ran the test two times. The first time, they found it to be inconclusive because the samples were checked against trees only known to be in the area. The second time, the technician ran the test she ran it against a larger database and found a match.

The splinters came from a wood that is classified as Swietenia Mahagoni. Or more commonly known as American mahogany. Kerry didn't need to read further to know that the wood was not native to Lake Pines. Builders rarely use wood that wasn't from the area, especially since the mill in the town supplied eighty percent of the jobs for the families of Lake Pines.

The report also showed the wood to be close to twenty-five years old, this the technician determined due to the levels of mold growth in the wood.

"So, who would have twenty-five-year-old American mahogany?" Kerry asked herself. She knew that it was unlikely to be anything other than a door or piece of furniture, and decided to begin her search there since there was little else to go on at the moment.

She searched for manufacturers of American mahogany furniture from twenty-five years ago. Her database returned sixty-three results.

"Oh, boy," Kerry muttered.

She narrowed her search to companies that sold to stores or customers in Canada at the time.

The search returned a more narrowed list of forty-five companies.

"Hmm," Kerry tapped away at her keyboard filtering the results to companies that dealt with the Northwestern Ontario region.

The cursor blinked for twenty seconds as the database filtered the results down to three.

Kerry smiled. Three she could handle.

Kerry punched the name of the first company in her browser and found it had been out of business for almost a decade.

The second company Kerry selected had an extremely basic website, but Kerry was still able to locate their phone number and contact name on their site.

After two rings a melodic voice answered the line, "Hellowwww, FGA Wood Products. How can I help you?" The young voice asked.

"Hello, my name is Doctor Dearborne. I'm calling from Lake Pines Coroner's Office, and I'm looking for an order that you may have filled around twenty-five years ago," Kerry explained.

"Hmm, that's a long time ago, dear. And I am not sure I can give out just any customer name," the girl said.

"I understand. But this is for a murder case I am working on. My name is Doctor Dearborne and I am investigating a murder that took place sometime this past fall and whoever may have purchased some of your furniture may give us a clue as to where our victim died."

"Oh, I see. Well, I can have Mr. Wilson contact you. He is the owner and he'd know where all those files are kept."

"That would be great, thank you."

Kerry gave the young girl her information, including her email and cell number, and told her that her boss could call any time of the day or night.

She giggled and then disconnected the line.

Kerry keyed in the last company name but as with the first contact, this one was out of business. Kerry would just have to patiently wait to see what Mr. Wilson from FGA Wood Products would have to say.

She then turned her attention to the results of the skin tissue found beneath the victim's nails. The technician ran the test and was unable to come up with a match for any DNA. She was, however, able to determine that there were traces of essential oil. It wasn't present on the victim's body, so it most definitely was sure to have been only on the attacker's skin.

The test revealed that the chemical composition determined the essential oil was patchouli. It wasn't a plant that grew naturally in Lake Pines. In fact, it was more commonly found in areas of South East Asia, and was often added to some skincare products. Any information in the case was important, but Kerry knew this alone was not going to be able to help her find the killer.

Kerry worked for another ten minutes and then a second email came into her inbox and this time it was regarding the black fiber that Kerry found inside the victim's ear.

Kerry pulled out her phone and pushed redial on the number that Wayne called her on this morning, and he answered on the first ring. She didn't have a lot of faith in Wayne, but he was the officer in charge, and she didn't want to jeopardize the case by not following the proper steps of authority.

"Doctor Dearborne, everything alright?" Wayne asked.

"I got the report back on the fiber from the victim's ear and it is from a foam insert for the earpiece of headphones," Kerry explained.

"Okay. . ." Wayne said, obviously not following Kerry's line of thinking.

"We didn't find a headset or a portable music device at the scene. If we can find it maybe, we can trace who the victim is. Those devices hook up to computers and might have some sort of tracker on it," Kerry explained.

Wayne was silent for a few seconds, "That's a great idea Doctor Dearborne. I am on my way out of town right now, but I'll get one of my junior officers up there right away to check the area. With all the rain we had today it might be difficult to search, but we will give it a try."

Kerry thanked Wayne and then disconnected the call. She decided not to tell Wayne about the wood until she had more information plus, she didn't even know if it would lead anywhere.

She sat back in her chair and looked out of the small window in her office that faced the lawn that rolled down to the lake. The rain had stopped, and strings of light were piercing through the clouds that still hovered in the sky. It was close to four in the afternoon and Kerry knew the sun would set soon and it would be almost impossible to search the area properly. That is, unless she got there before dark.

9

Kerry grabbed her coat and her rubber boots and left her office. Without any staff, Kerry didn't have to explain to anyone where she was going, so she just locked the office and left.

She parked at the far end of the trails to Tunnel Island and entered from the backside. She knew it was rockier, that way she could avoid stirring up too much mud walking into the area which was still cordoned off with police tape.

Kerry reached the area and found some of the yellow police barricade tape had been ripped down. It was either curious kids from town or a deer that was innocently roaming the area searching for food. Kerry knew it was a long shot, but she turned on her flashlight and worked her way back and forth across the area with her eyes scanning the ground. Peter had taught Kerry an efficient and quick way to search an area for evidence, and she used it every time.

"But never rush," Peter would remind her when she started to get too ahead of herself with excitement.

As she suspected, the area became dark rather quickly and with the sun setting and the dampness in the air from the heavy rain, Kerry felt a chill start to settle in. Her raincoat was great for keeping her dry but not for keeping her warm, and she began to shiver.

Kerry reached the area where she tripped over the victim's foot and felt heartbroken. She could only imagine how the young girl felt before she died, knowing she had a baby waiting for her. If it wasn't for the fact that Kerry found a body on this trail, she would have thought the view was spectacular tonight in the light of dusk.

Kerry returned her focus to the trail and tried to figure out the path that the killer would have taken if he, or she, were to drag a body into this area to bury. She shone her flashlight around a cluster of branches that had fallen to the ground and then she heard sounds coming toward her.

Kerry didn't have time to hide before the first man walked around a clump of trees and spotted her bright yellow raincoat. He was over twenty feet away and with dusk setting in, it was difficult to see his face.

Kerry was just about to announce she was with the coroner's office when he shouted and raised his arm toward her. Kerry saw the gun in his hand, and she ran for cover.

"Over here!" a muffled yell came from the man with the gun as he turned to his partner. Kerry heard his steps as he turned around to chase her. The mix of mud and branches created a strange sound as his boots sunk into the sopping ground.

"Don't let her go," the second man yelled as he, too, began to give chase.

Kerry sprinted around trees and rocks and wove her way toward the edge of the water and jumped over a small hill that dipped down to the lake.

She switched off her flashlight and ducked behind a large clump of birch trees near the edge of the water. She could hear branches snapping as two men approached. There were definitely two people, both men, and they were running as they spoke. She couldn't make out what they were saying but she could tell by the movement of the shadows of their bodies, that they were searching for her.

"Over there," she thought she heard one man yell to the other.

The voices grew closer as they stepped nearer to where Kerry was hiding. Thunder began to rumble in the distance and a cool wind blew up from the water and Kerry felt the gust begin to push against her back.

The mens' steps were getting closer and Kerry crouched down on the rocks to keep her bright yellow raincoat from being seen by one of their roving flashlights.

"Where was she buried?" the second man asked the first, no longer referring to Kerry.

The thunder grew louder, and each rumbling was getting closer together and soon rain began to pelt down through the trees. The wind picked up and began to blow the rain into the forest and against Kerry's body. Her hands, cold with the night chill, began to slip from the branches she was holding onto as she crouched low on the rocks. Icy beads of rain pelted her exposed skin, stinging the surface with each hit.

As the men moved closer, Kerry tried to move her body further away from sight and her rubber boots began to slide against the rocks now slippery with the rain. Her boots gave way and she began to slide down toward the water and the branch she was clinging to slipped through her fingers until it snapped up and out of her grip.

Kerry's fall sent her crashing against a large boulder that stopped her body from plunging into the icy cold water. She lay motionless and looked up toward the top of the small hill and watched the glimmer of the flashlights roll through the darkness. She was no longer able to hear their voices over the thunder and pounding rain, however, she watched as the lights waved from side to side and then straight up in the air before they headed back out of the forest.

Pain radiated through her ribs as she shifted her body. Kerry stiffened at the slightest movement as she tried to stand from where she fell hard against the rock.

She clawed her way to the top of the hill grabbing random branches and digging her fingers into crevices in the rocks until she reached the muddy pinnacle.

Aware that she was not going to find anything now that the heavy rain had started, Kerry, headed back toward where she parked her car. Away from the men who had just left, and away from any chance at finding more evidence at the victim's burial site.

Wayne handed Simon one of the sticks he grabbed on the way out of the forest as they stumbled over the rocks, slippery from the heavy rain. Simon leaned against the side of his truck and tried his best to dig out the heavy mud that clung to the bottom of his boots and was packed into the deep ridged treads. His shivering hands fumbled with the small stick he pushed against the bottom of his boot.

After a few snapped sticks and five minutes, Simon and Wayne gave up under the assault of heavy rain that pounded down and soaked them. Even the thick outer layer of their hunting coats failed to keep them dry.

With mud still firmly lodged in their boots, they climbed into the cab of Simon's truck and pulled out onto the road, and drove toward town in the dark. Hoping they hadn't been seen.

10

Cold, damp air, like an icy blanket, draped itself around Kerry as she stepped out of her house. It was seven a.m. and Kerry had been fighting off a headache for hours that hammered her head and refused to let her sleep. She figured a quick run then a shower should get her blood pumping and help her focus. An hour and a half later Kerry acquiesced and took two aspirin with her third mug of coffee.

Kerry had arrived at a dark house the night before and no message from Simon.

She thought back to their argument at the museum and wondered if they could get past it and if she ever would have a chance to try and convince Simon to move to Montreal with her. Kerry ran a hot bath and submersed herself under the foam of bubbles. Her back ached from where she collided with the rock and after she made it home, she realized she had also twisted her knee and tore her raincoat. She tossed the coat in the garbage, poured a tea, and tried to ignore the fact that she wished Simon was with her.

She soaked in the bath until the water began to lose heat, and with her hands wrapped around a hot mug of tea, she crawled into bed and tucked the thick down duvet around her body. Kerry fell into a deep slumber until three a.m. when she was awoken by a pounding headache and the thought of her young victim and what her last few days must have been like. Once her thoughts moved to the fact that her victim was also a mother, Kerry had given up the idea of more sleep.

She rose from her empty bed and after a long hot shower, she left for her office, where being alone was a choice.

* * *

Ordinarily, Kerry preferred the temperature in the office to be a little on the cool side, however, today she slid the tab on the thermostat an extra ten degrees, and within twenty minutes the chill was removed from the air as well as her body.

The lack of success in obtaining any further evidence in the forest frustrated

Kerry. However, she was more curious about the two men who arrived after she did.

It was obvious that they were also looking for something at the site, and whoever it was more than likely had something to do with the victim's death. Kerry learned from her years working as a coroner, that coincidences were rare.

Her mind went to her conversation with Wayne and although she didn't want to admit it, he was the only person who knew that there may have been something at the site to find. That, along with the fact that the list he gave her for the hospitals was altered, made it difficult to trust him.

She picked up the phone and dialed the station and asked to be put through to Officer Jones.

After a short, friendly chat with the receptionist, the pleasant Officer Jones was on the line, "Officer Jones speaking. How may I help you?"

"Good morning, Officer Jones. It's Doctor Dearborne," Kerry greeted him.

"Good morning Doctor Dearborne. How did your search turn out?" he asked.

"Pardon?"

"The hospital list I gave you. Did you get any helpful information?"

"Oh, that. I am waiting to hear back from the supervisor of the department. It seems as if the nurse on duty the night the baby was born has since retired," Kerry explained. "Actually, I am calling because of something else. Last night I was out at the site where the body was found, and there were two suspicious men also there at the site."

"Suspicious how?" Officer Jones asked.

"Well for starters, they had pointed a gun at me and then chased me to the edge of the water," Kerry recalled.

"Did you get a look at them?" Officer Jones asked.

"No, it was getting dark and the light was fading. I did however hear some of what they were saying, and it seems as if they were looking for something. Maybe the same thing I was looking for," Kerry said, realizing how vague she sounded.

"And what would that be?" Officer Jones asked.

"I think the victim may have had a portable music device with her when she was killed, and since it wasn't on her body when we exhumed her, it may have fallen off when she was transported from where she was killed," Kerry explained.

"I see," Officer Jones said.

"I called Constable Burgess last night and he said he was going to have an officer go out and check. Do you know if he did that?" Kerry asked.

"Yes, he left a message for me, but I didn't get it until after it started to rain so I went by this morning and I wasn't able to find anything. I am going to send out two officers this afternoon with a metal detector to have a go at it," Officer Jones said.

"Great, thanks."

"No problem Doctor Dearborne. If you have any other questions, just give me a call. Constable Burgess won't be back in the office for a few days," Officer Jones added.

"Why? Where is he?" Kerry asked.

"I thought you would have known since he is with Simon. He said he would be out at his cabin for the next few days."

Kerry was stunned that Wayne and Simon had left for a few days and neither thought to mention it to her. She thanked Officer Jones and ended the call before her upset became obvious.

Kerry flipped through her files and emails but still had no further contact from the furniture company in Florida. She decided to take another look at the hospital list that Officer Jones had given her and compared them once again to the list that Wayne Burgess had on his desk.

When Kerry had finished going through the list one final time, she had highlighted three extra entries on the list.

She systematically called each hospital and spoke directly with the supervisors and except for the hospital in Thunder Bay, everyone was able to confirm that the mothers who gave birth over the last year either did not match the description of the victim or had a recent checkup and could be confirmed safe.

Putting a name to every unidentified body that came through her office was non-negotiable for Kerry. Jean had thought that is what lead to her stress leave when she left Montreal many years ago. He tried to tell her that just sometimes you must accept there was no answer.

Kerry didn't believe that, nor did she want to accept it.

She located the phone number and name of the supervisor in Thunder Bay and punched the numbers for his direct line.

"Hello, Doctor Madison speaking," his voice was deep, but not intimidating or harsh. If Kerry had to guess, she would have said Doctor Madison was close to Jean's age and maybe even close to retirement.

"Hello Doctor Madison, it's Doctor Dearborne calling. From Lake Pines Coroner's Office," Kerry said.

"Ah yes. I see there is a message here to call you. It seems you want to rule out a patient of ours as your victim," he said.

"Or confirm it," Kerry said in response.

"Yes, it is very unfortunate when young people's lives end so suddenly. However, I am sorry, but without a warrant, I'm unable to release any information on any of our patients. Even if it is as serious as your case is," Doctor Madison explained.

"Could you just confirm if your patient is alive? Even if you were to call her yourself?" Kerry asked.

"No, I am sorry. But if you get a warrant . . ."

"Yes, I understand. I just don't know how long that will take. Things tend to move quite slowly here in Lake Pines," Kerry explained hoping to gain some sympathy.

The doctor apologized and reassured Kerry that if she were to obtain the proper warrant and paperwork, he would personally expedite the file. In fact, he promised to keep the file on his desk so she wouldn't have to wait much longer. Kerry sat at her desk with her phone now disconnected and lying flat on the table. She thought back to all the times she was in a similar situation in Montreal and how she was able to bypass the regulations. Kerry knew that was a lot easier because she was able to physically appear in the hospital or doctor's office, making it harder for anyone to blow her off.

Kerry looked at her calendar and stared at the large block of white that covered her schedule. There was no point in hanging around when she had a chance of sorting out the matter of who her victim was.

She grabbed her keys and coat and headed for her Jeep. She paused at the door when Simon's number flashed up on her screen, and pressed a button to send his call to her voicemail. His call and the conversation would have to wait until she was ready. Kerry slipped the phone into her pocket, and left for Thunder Bay, where she hoped would get some answers.

11

Thunder Bay was only a few short hours away, but the drive seemed to go faster as Kerry preoccupied her thoughts with her unidentified victim, her relationship with Simon, and her job offer from Jean. The winding highway carved its way through thick strips of Canadian Shield and past lakes and valleys that rested alongside the road. It wasn't a highway that you could drive without being consumed with the beauty of the landscape. It didn't seem to matter what the season was, when Kerry drove along the TransCanada, it always amazed her at how beautiful the countryside was.

Kerry was rounding a bend and began her descent when she spotted Thunder Bay in the distance. She didn't need a headcount to know that it was triple the size of Lake Pines. She was even able to identify an area that was designated as the downtown from the distance on top of the hill as she made her way into the city.

A mix of hotels and motels lined the road into town and randomly popped up through the city as she made her way toward the hospital. She would need neither on this trip, but she remembered staying at the Mountain Inn when she drove out with Simon one February when he wanted to show her the ski hill in the area. She didn't have the heart to tell him that she was a proficient skier, having learned to ski on the famed, and sometimes icy, Laurentian Mountains in Quebec. However, once she dropped from the ski lift it was hard to hide her skill and she laughed at the shock on Simon's face when she raced past him as he stood near the tree line for her to catch up to him. The rest of the day they tackled one run after the other until their legs finally gave out and they agreed to spend the rest of the evening in the hot tub with a glass of wine.

Kerry shook the memory from her head and focused on which direction she was driving as she made her way toward the hospital. The large white cross was visible from the outskirts of the city, however, the closer she got, she had to rely on her sense of direction to guide her toward her destination.

Kerry pulled into the visitor parking lot, grabbed a ticket from the dispenser, and slipped her Jeep into the last spot in the lot. She had only a slim file with her and although she had forwarded the information to Doctor Madison through email, she thought the visual of having the paperwork in her hands would be a good strategic move.

She went directly to the directory that screwed to the side of the wall and bypassed the security guard altogether. Doctor Madison was located on the second floor in room 236.

Kerry walked up the one flight of stairs and exited on the second floor across from the nurses' station. She pulled out her Provincial credentials badge that hung from around her neck on a lanyard, and let it dangle in front of her sweater.

Three nurses sat behind the administrative desk. The first nurse she spotted was a woman in her fifties and she carried the air of a seasoned professional. Her hair was neatly pinned into a bun, and her plain blue scrubs showed practicality as Kerry knew they were hospital-supplied ones that saved the nurse from frequent washes and extra money otherwise spent on patterned scrubs. Kerry's instincts told her that this nurse would be one that would lean toward wanting official paperwork before she released any patient information.

A younger man stood behind the desk and was organizing the patient board hanging on the wall. A whiteboard listed the names of each patient along with the nurse's notes at each shift change. He wore his hair short and had a stylish growth of stubble on his face that seemed intentional and not because of lack of time. A row of small studs dotted the edge of his ears and a black decorative tattoo crawled from under the sleeve of his uniform and along his muscular forearm. He possessed the strength necessary to deal with heavier patients, but his body language and facial expressions displayed he had a gentler demeanor than his more senior coworker.

Seated at the counter was a young girl in pink scrubs with a pattern of daisies over them whose badge displayed she was still in training.

Kerry waited for the young male nurse to complete his task organizing the patients on the floor, and for the more senior nurse to make her way down the hall and into the rooms of one of her patients. He turned around and saw Kerry standing at the counter and after he glanced at the badge that hung from around her neck he asked if he could help her.

Kerry placed the file folder on the counter and intentionally let the official Lake Pines Coroner logo sit face up, "I'm looking for some information on a patient who would have been through here almost a year ago. I need it to help me identify a victim."

"What information do you have?" He asked, glancing at the file folder in front of him.

"Not much I'm afraid. Just that she would have received a cesarean section at the time," Kerry explained.

Before the nurse could respond, or Kerry could explain further, a voice beamed from behind her.

"Doctor Dearborne, I presume," the voice was deep, warm, and familiar and belonged to Doctor Madison.

Kerry twisted around and was looking into the face of the doctor she was speaking with this morning and was unwilling to release any of the patient's information over the phone.

"Hello, Doctor Madison," Kerry thrust out her hand to greet him. "I was going to be in the area and thought I would just pop in and see if I could get the ball rolling."

"Really?" Doctor Madison folded his arms across his chest, and instead of looking stern, he smiled.

"Okay," Kerry confessed. "Maybe I'm in the area *because* I need to find out some answers. And I can't wait for the court to sign an official warrant or order for you. I know my victim has had a child and even though we haven't been able to determine who her killer was, I want to at least be able to give her family some closure. You have no idea how slowly some things move in Lake Pines. It could be a couple of weeks before I have any order signed for you."

Doctor Madison chuckled, "You think it's bad where you are, you should have seen how bad it was when I started my career in Montreal. It could take weeks to get any necessary paperwork and then by that time, it often was too late."

"You worked in Montreal?" Kerry stepped closer to Doctor Madison.

"Yes, when I first graduated. But that was a long time ago," Doctor Madison explained. He began to walk down the hall and Kerry followed beside him as he spoke.

"It was hard to wrap my head around the fact that I had to wait for some bureaucrat to sign a simple document just for me to do my job. And I wasn't the criminal!"

"You didn't work with Doctor Jean Lamont, by any chance?" Kerry asked. Montreal was a big city, but the medical community was small enough that doctors the same age all knew each other. And it didn't take long to assess Doctor Madison to be the same age as Jean.

"Why yes, I did!" Doctor Madison answered, with a bit of excitement in his voice. "How do you know Jean?"

"I was his protégé, you could say," Kerry beamed.

Doctor Madison turned left and walked into a corner office at the end of the hall. The carpet was threadbare, and the walls painted a faded hospital green that was the color of choice in the seventies. The government presumed it relaxed patients, but Kerry thought it just felt cold and unwelcoming. His desk was like the one Kerry had in her coroner's office in Lake Pines. It was a regulation metal desk painted a slate grey and had a top of padded black vinyl. A small slim computer was the only indication of modernization in the office.

Doctor Madison stretched out his hand and motioned for Kerry to sit in one of the chairs across from his desk. He pulled out the high back black leather office chair and sat down. He grabbed the edge of the desk, pulling his chair forward, and his legs disappeared underneath.

"Ah yes, then you were trained with the same tenacity that Jean is famous for," Doctor Madison laughed. He switched on his computer and began to type his seven-digit security code across the keyboard. Kerry could see he was proficient at typing and she hoped it also meant he kept organized records.

"Let's see if we can get you some information without divulging any patient confidentiality," Doctor Madison said.

Kerry breathed a sigh of relief and opened the file folder she held in her hands, although she knew the particulars off the top of her head, "Well the victim is between twenty-five and thirty, sandy blonde hair, blue eyes, and had a baby approximately ten months ago," Kerry read from her examination file.

"Well our patient does match all of those characteristics," Doctor Madison confirmed. "How did you come about your assertion that she had the baby about ten months ago?"

"By the degree of healing in her cesarean scar," Kerry said.

"Oh, well that helps," Doctor Madison said.

"So, your patient could be my victim then," Kerry was glad her trip was not in vain.

"No, I am sorry. Our patient didn't have a surgical birth when she delivered her baby," Doctor Madison was apologetic but also happy that one of his patients was not Kerry's victim.

After thanking Doctor Madison for his time, Kerry struck the final name off her list, and she promised to say hello to Jean for him.

She left his office, thanked the male nurse at the nurses' station and climbed down the stairs, and walked out of the hospital. She was within eyeshot of her Jeep when the voice mail alert buzzed on her phone. Kerry played the message hoping it was Simon so they could start to work things out. The drive made her remember that their relationship held enough good memories that it was worth working at saving. Instead, it was Officer Jones who was calling to confirm that the officers he sent out with a metal detector hadn't found anything at the site.

Kerry was back to square one and the victim was no closer to having a name than the day Kerry found her.

And her family was going to have to go another day without knowing why she wasn't coming home.

12

Kerry was twenty minutes from Lake Pines town limits when she spotted a roadside diner that she and Simon stopped at when they were returning home from their ski trip a year and a half ago. She pulled into the parking lot and stepped out of her Jeep to stretch her arms and arch her back to release some of the tension that had built up over the long drive.

Kerry was unable to occupy her mind the way she did when she drove out earlier that day, and consequently, the drive back to Lake Pines seemed much longer. Kerry thought she'd grab a coffee and when the aroma of the diner hit her, her stomach began to growl.

She walked toward the entrance and pulled the door open, standing aside to let an elderly couple walk out. Just before she was about to step inside, she spotted Simon sitting in a booth along the backside of the diner. He was deep in conversation and hadn't noticed Kerry standing at the entrance.

Across from him sat a beautiful woman who held physical attributes that Kerry did not. She had long blonde hair pinned up into a messy bun that fell along the right side of her face. Her blue eyes were noticeable from across the room and her petite figure stood in contrast to the enormity of the meal that filled the plate in front of her.

Kerry turned and walked back to her Jeep without acknowledging Simon or the girl sitting across from him.

As Kerry backed her Jeep out of the lot, she could still see Simon sitting on the stool, deep in conversation, and unaware that Kerry was just there.

Kerry pulled out of the lot and onto the highway and headed back to town. Leaving her hopes for a reconciliation with Simon behind.

13

Some days Kerry found the disappointment at work too hard to deal with and needed to just get out of the office. Today was one of those days. She would usually have Simon to talk to and because her cases could sometimes be unsettling for most people, she never spoke about them with any of her friends. Today, Kerry was left to work out her frustration on her own. She couldn't understand if Wayne was just incompetent or if he was intentionally trying to sabotage the case. Either way, it left Kerry feeling helpless and frustrated.

Kerry drove down to the boatyard to speak with Jim about her boat. She had been putting off selling her boat until she was positive she was ready to leave Lake Pines. Jim Chandler ran the Lake Pines Marina and was the one who had sold her the boat in the first place. Jim started working at Lake Pines Marina when he was sixteen pumping gas and performing minor repairs to boats that would come in with dings and missing cleats. After a while, the owner realized that Jim had an innate mechanical talent and had encouraged him to take some courses on boat engine repair during the winter months so he could give him more work. A year later Jim oversaw all engine repairs that came through the marina and over time he bought the business from his boss who was looking to retire. When Kerry was looking for a boat, Jim sold her the 1970 Grew he had rebuilt after a cottager ran it up on the shore.

Kerry loved the space the boat offered. She was more comfortable driving a large boat and worried less at the prospect of hitting underwater rocks. She didn't like the idea of parting with the boat, however, if she was to move to Montreal, she wouldn't have any need for it there.

The chill hung in the air from the twenty hours of heavy rain, but now the sun shone bright and danced on the water that moved with each small wave. At the last moment, Kerry decided to leave her Jeep parked at her office. The walk was a short one from her office and the day was mild and it would give her a chance to loosen her back from the long drive.

Kerry could hear the radio playing in Jim's workshop as she walked closer to the marina. The clanging of gears echoed off the cement floor as Jim tossed and changed the wrenches and tools he was using on the raised engine.

Like most of the people Kerry became close to in Lake Pines, Jim had also gone to the same school as Simon did. Which was easy to do with only two schools in town. It occurred to Kerry that even if she stayed, if she was unable to work things out with Simon, it would be extremely awkward to socialize with any of their friends. Even though Kerry grew close to them, they were his friends first.

"Hi Jim," Kerry bent down and peered under the raised engine that Jim was working on.

Jim smiled at the sound of Kerry's voice and dropped the wrench he held in his hand and crawled out from underneath the engine. He wiped the grease from his hands on a rag and walked over to the table and turned down the sound on the radio.

Jim had the type of personality that everyone immediately warmed to. He gave you the feeling that you knew him much longer than you did. He had kindness in his eyes that you sensed the instant you met him, and an infectious laugh and a kind heart. Jim was the 'swizzle stick' in the group of friends that he and Simon grew up with. He was the reason people with little in common remained friends and was usually the one that planned their social events.

"Hey Kerry, what's up?" Jim pulled off his 'lakes are for fishing' hat and pulled his thick fingers through his long brown hair and then slipped his hat back on his head. This time placing it backward like a teenager.

"What are you working on?" Kerry asked pointing at the indescribable machine Jim had up on a hoist.

"Oh that," Jim waived off the pile of metal and engine suspended from the ceiling with chains. "I am designing a go-cart boat for my nephew for his birthday this summer. It'll be a one of a kind."

"Cool. I have never heard of a go-cart boat," Kerry laughed.

"It's because it doesn't exist. Who knows, maybe I can sell them," Jim shrugged. Along with boat engine repairs, he was known as the guy who could build anything. If you wanted something with an engine, Jim could build it. And if you needed it to be waterborne, then he was the only one in town who could build it.

"Jim, I wanted to talk to you about the Grew," Kerry began.

"Do you want it tuned up early this spring?" Jim asked.

"Not exactly," Kerry explained. "I wanted to talk to you about selling it."

Jim raised both his eyebrows and widened his eyes, "Why? I hope it wasn't giving you any trouble last season."

"No, the boat is great. I love it, actually," Kerry smiled. She didn't know how much to say to Jim, and she didn't want to bring up Montreal and cause more of an issue between her and Simon. "I just may want to sell it this year and I know that the spring is a good time to think about putting it up for sale."

Jim shoved both of his hands in his pockets, "You've got that right." Jim rubbed his chin with his hand while he thought over an idea in his head. "Look, I'll keep an ear out for anyone looking for a boat that size, but I will keep you informed of any interest before I accept an offer, just in case you change your mind. I can always yank it back from a buyer by telling them something is up with the engine. I would hate to see you lose such a great boat."

Kerry smiled and fought to hold back tears that began to fill her eyes. She slipped her sunglasses on her face to hide them, "Thanks, Jim. I knew I could count on you."

Kerry turned to leave before Jim could ask any further questions when he called her name.

"I have something for Simon. If you wait, I can give it to you," Jim ran to the back room and after a few minutes he reappeared with a set of golf clubs wrapped inside his arms.

"These are my brother-in-law's, but he is never going to use them. He sucks at golf and after last year he said he was never going to take it up. Which is probably a good thing," Jim laughed. "Anyway, I told Simon he could have them."

Kerry took the bag, "They look expensive. Are you sure you don't want them?"

"Nah, I can't use them because they are left-handed clubs."

Kerry walked out of the marina and back toward her office wincing at the pain in her back. The fall bruised her ribs and now with the weight of carrying the golf clubs, each step brought a searing stab of pain to her body.

Kerry stopped and began to walk back toward the marina thinking she should ask Jim to keep the idea of selling the Grew to himself. Small towns had a way of sharing news unintentionally, and Kerry didn't want to field any prodding questions about why she was selling the boat. Especially after spotting him yesterday at the diner.

She walked along the dock and rounded the corner into Jim's workshop, where she left him moments ago. A large man stood next to Jim, but just far enough to Jim's left that his face was blocked by a post.

His voice was unfamiliar, and he had an American accent that she just couldn't place. He was a heavy-set man, fully dressed in black. Their voices were raised in a disagreeable tone, giving a hint of an argument.

"I need this thing finished tomorrow," the large man in black demanded. "No more delays. Got it."

Jim promised his customer that he would work late into the evening to finish the work, and he would call the moment he was done.

"And no later," the man snapped as he walked past Jim shoving him to the side as he went.

Jim deserved his privacy, even with the jerk of a customer that just left his marina. Jim was a proud man and would've been embarrassed to know that

Kerry witnessed a customer chewing him out over a delay.

Kerry hoisted the clubs over her shoulder and wincing under the pain, she walked up the road.

Kerry opened the back of her Jeep and placed the clubs inside and slammed the back door shut.

14

Simon tossed his bag and his coat on the floor in the corner and slumped down on the sofa. He had burst through the door a short while after Kerry returned home from work and was in a panic to speak with her. His boots were covered in mud that had dried and was now flaking off onto the rug. She suppressed the pull she had to ask him who he was meeting with at the diner, unsure of wanting to explain why she was there in the first place, thinking he would not believe her, and they would get into another argument.

Kerry also fought the urge to ask him to remove his boots, not wanting to add tension to his mood. They had not spoken since their argument in the museum and Kerry didn't want to leave their relationship with the memory of a fight between them.

Jim had called Simon when Kerry had left the marina to let him know that he had given Kerry the golf clubs and to arrange a time for them both to go to the driving range so they would be ready to hit the course when the snow had melted and the course had dried. At some point in the conversation, Jim had mentioned that it was too bad that Kerry was thinking of selling the Grew. It was an innocent comment, but enough to worry Simon.

"He teased me that maybe we were thinking of getting married and getting a new boat together," Simon sounded upset.

The topic was now thrown in her face and Kerry couldn't avoid the conversation any longer. In a way, she was happy her hand was forced. She wanted to explain what had preoccupied her mind over the last several months. Kerry took a deep breath and began to explain everything to Simon.

"I got a call from Jean," Kerry began. "He offered me a job."

Simon stared at her, stunned.

"Say something," Kerry pleaded. His silence was more painful than their fights.

"When?" Simon asked. "When did Jean call?"

"A few weeks ago," Kerry lied.

Simon buried his face in his hands and sighed, "And you are just telling me now? I thought we were a team?"

"So, did I," Kerry said. "But since last summer you have seemed distant, and you disappear almost every weekend with Wayne." The memory of Simon in the diner yesterday flashed in her mind and she decided to stay silent. It wouldn't be the reason she would leave anyway.

"This is about Wayne now?" Simon snapped.

"No," Kerry calmed her voice. "I am just saying, I haven't felt that you really want to be here. With me."

"Well I'm here now," Simon said. He held his hands wide, stretching across the width of the sofa.

Kerry explained Jean's offer and that she hadn't said anything to Simon because she wasn't sure she was even going to consider it. However, recently she started to think it was the only way she was going to be able to save her career.

"I was just thinking I should see if there was any interest in the boat. Just in case I did take the job in Montreal," Kerry explained about the boat, hoping to calm Simon's mood.

"So, you *are* considering it?" Simon asked.

"I think so. But I don't want to go without working things out with you," Kerry added.

"My life is here Kerry," Simon's voice began to waver.

"And I'm finding that my career has hit a dead-end here in Lake Pines. And plus, working with Wayne is becoming impossible."

"Did you ever think that maybe you are the one being impossible?" Simon snapped, "Ever since Peter left you haven't given Wayne a chance."

Simon stood up, grabbed his coat, and stormed out of the house, leaving a trail of dried mud in his wake. Kerry didn't have the energy to follow him out and endure another argument. Especially one that may involve him supporting Wayne since she wasn't even sure that she could trust him.

Kerry took a deep breath and relaxed her shoulders. That was the hardest part. Now all she had to do was wait to see how Simon felt after he calmed down and they were able to talk a little more about a possible move.

Kerry grabbed the broom and swept the dried mud toward the back hall. She grabbed a dustpan and collected the dried debris with a few swift sweeps and brought it to the laundry room. After she dumped the dirt into the empty trash can, she grabbed Simon's bag and walked it into the laundry room.

As she tossed it on the floor a loud clunk echoed as a side pocket opened and several items spilled out onto the floor. As Kerry began to pick up the items that lay on the floor a slight chill ran through her spine.

Simon's phone fell out and text alerts flashed across his screen. They were from Wayne and Kerry froze in place as she read the last one.

"Don't tell Kerry we were up at the lodge. With everything going on I don't need her on my back, and you don't need the grief."

Kerry slipped the phone back into Simon's bag's side pocket and rested it against the bench.

She scooped up the clothes that fell to the ground and dropped them in the laundry basket. There was a familiar scent she noticed in Simon's clothes that made her remember their time at Fox Lodge. She pulled out the dirt-stained towel and tossed it in the open washing machine deciding to wash it separately from the clothes. Kerry glanced down and under the pile of clothes and towels was the old buck knife Simon's father gave him lying on the floor, and the handle was discolored with dried blood.

15

Kerry focused the handle of the buck knife under the microscope and adjusted the zoom lens. Most of the blade had been wiped clean and traces of dried blood remained in the grooves of the handle and in the markings on the blade. The traces were so small and only were present in the narrow grooves of the handle's design and the imprint on the blade. Over time there would've been numerous traces of blood and grit on Simon's hunting gear, but it would belong to animals, not humans. Kerry pulled her face away from the microscope and rubbed her face with the palms of her hands. When she dropped the knife in a bag at home, she had told herself that she was just going to check the knife so that way if she was able to find the real murder weapon, she would know what to look for. She continued to convince herself of the same motivation the whole drive to her office. Now that she sat in front of the microscope, a wave of guilt took over and she pulled the blade from under the lens. There was no way Simon could have been responsible for such a horrible crime. Many people were left-handed that also owned hunting knives in Lake Pines.

The knife was a gift from his father when he was young, and it held a lot of special memories for him. He always took it with him when he went to the cottage or out on a fishing or hunting trip with his friends. She was aware that she was letting her feelings for Simon creep into her doubts about him and her concern over not being able to give her victim a name.

When Kerry first arrived in Lake Pines, and when her budget was much larger, she purchased a soil tester for her office. She had used it many times and had found it came in handy when she needed to narrow down a location where a body was found, murdered or if a suspect had been there. Today she was using it to compare the sample on Simon's boots to samples from the site where the victim was found. She set the samples in the tester and started the machine. It whirred as the mud, each in its own slurry, was spinning inside two glass vials. The particles were broken down so they could be easily read and compared. The test usually took an hour, so Kerry set the timer and returned to her desk.

She wanted to push aside her suspicions of Simon. Maybe he was right. She wasn't giving anyone the benefit of the doubt. Especially Wayne. She was so confused. Kerry returned the knife to the bag and dropped it into her desk drawer and slammed it shut.

She grabbed her lab coat, tape recorder, and gloves and went into the examining room to complete the autopsy on Mr. Roberts who was found slumped in his easy chair the night before last. Mr. Roberts had reached the age of ninety-four without the need for living assistance or medication. He took little prompting to share this fact along with the secret to his amazing health when Kerry would see him in town.

"A good brisk walk every morning and night," Mr. Roberts would explain. "And a shot of whiskey before bed." At this point, he would laugh and shoot Kerry a wink. Mr. Roberts was a warm-hearted fixture in Lake Pines and was the principal at one of the two local schools. His warm smile was always ready for anyone who stopped to chat with him, and his level of compassion astounded everyone who knew him. From offering shelter to children who had run away from home so they would have a safe place to sleep until they could smooth things over, to volunteering at the community center where he tutored children with their studies. Mr. Roberts had time enough for everyone, and his daughter had said that is why God gave him extra time on Earth. To pay him back for all he gave.

Kerry was sure Mr. Roberts had died of natural causes and was probably laughing down at her from above, daring her to find something wrong. Two hours later Kerry was finished her report and concluded that Mr. Roberts indeed passed away in his sleep of a silent heart attack.

She took extra time to help prep his body for delivery to the funeral director, wanting to give him all the respect his life deserved.

By the time she was back at her computer, it was late afternoon and Kerry was pleased the day passed as quickly as it did.

It wasn't until she walked past the soil testing machine that she remembered she set it earlier to test the soil on Simon's boots. She pulled out the small strip of paper that recorded the sample findings and was now hanging from the slot on the side of the machine. She held it for a few minutes before she folded it in half and put it in the same drawer that she put Simon's knife in without reading it.

Kerry tapped away at her keyboard and pulled up her email and began to delete the unnecessary and spammy emails as she scanned her inbox hoping to find one that would help with identifying the victim found on Tunnel Island.

The third from the bottom was the email she was hoping to find. The sender was FGA Wood Products. She clicked the email open and found the receptionist, who she thought was not paying attention, had not only conveyed the correct information to her boss but had assembled a list of two customers from the area around Lake Pines. It appeared FGA was not as concerned with protecting their client's information as the staff at Thunder Bay hospital was.

Two clients had ordered hand-carved doors for their homes. One was for Maude and Gordon Scott and the other was for Geraldine and Raymond Fox. Their addresses were listed below their names, and although Kerry knew the owners would no longer be alive, it was only the location she was trying to find. And now she had them both.

* * *

742 Main Street was the home of Maude and Gordon Scott and Kerry had arrived a little after four-thirty. The sun was

setting on the street and Kerry pushed her sunglasses from where they rested on her nose to the top of her head. She didn't bother getting out of the car. Her view of the empty lot was clear from where she sat behind the wheel of her Jeep. The house at 742 Main had been demolished along with three on either side and a bare strip of land stretched along the street. Except for some garbage that blew into the lot and lodged itself against the fence, there was no sign of any structure on the property. By the looks of the ground, the foundations would have been filled in years ago, meaning the house would not have been standing the day her victim was taken.

Kerry looked at the next address on the list and put her car into drive and headed west to Caron Road. Geraldine and

Raymond Fox lived at 19 Caron Road. It was a large corner lot that bordered Canal Street. Kerry pulled up in front of the house and parked along the curb. She stepped out of her car and walked along the sidewalk until she reached the front walkway to the house. She was halfway up the path before she realized the damage that had taken place to the building. Burn marks curved from the top of the window frames where the flames of the fire escaped from the house. Charred and bubbled paint had flaked over the years and the roof shingles had curled and bent from where the heat melted the tar. Kerry walked around the building and was shocked to find the building still standing after she realized the damage on the backside was far worse than the front. Half of the building had fallen into itself and a gaping hole stood where the warmth of the family living room was, adjacent to the kitchen. Water and snow had damaged the remaining wood on the interior of the home, but Kerry could see there was not enough cover to hide the victim before she was killed. Either way, she would ask Wayne to get a team down here to examine the property. One way or another, Kerry was going to figure out if her victim was here with her killer.

It took Wayne less than forty minutes to gather the fire examiner and additional staff at 19 Caron Road. Kerry had to admit Wayne seemed to be taking her lead seriously. Maybe Simon was right, and she was being too hard on him. He had even brought a hot chocolate for her, which she drank while they waited.

It took the crew a full two hours to search and document the lot, but less than half an hour to determine that no murder had taken place at 19 Caron Road. The fire chief had told Kerry that the fire took place three years ago and the owners were in a protracted battle with the city to rezone the property. They wanted to build their dream home and that is why it had not been torn down yet. There wasn't one stable structure on the property and very little wood that survived the burn. Also, no blood was found by the search dogs, and a stab wound as severe as Kerry described would have left enough blood to be detected by the search dogs.

Kerry thanked Wayne and the fire chief and left them to finish up their report and she headed home. She pulled into Joe Blacks' coffee shop for a bag of beans for her coffee the next morning and was pleased to see it was still open and that there was a parking spot available right out front.

The door hit the hanging bell that was suspended over the door frame when Kerry pushed open the large glass door to the shop.

"Hello Kerry," Lisa, the young cashier, greeted her. "How are you?"

"Tired. And out of coffee for tomorrow morning," Kerry said.

"The usual?" Lisa asked.

"Of course," Kerry had been buying the same blend of coffee beans since she arrived in Lake Pines and brewed the same strength of coffee every day.

Kerry walked over to the shelf that Lisa had set up against a wall in the café that was lined with items from small artisans in Lake Pines.

"I see Mrs. Thorne coerced you into displaying some of her birdhouses," Kerry said.

Lisa laughed, "Try and say no to her. Actually, it gave me the idea to offer some shelf space to some other artisans selling their goods in exchange for a small percentage of their sales."

"That is nice of you," Kerry said.

"Well, it is a small way I can give back. Plus, I get the amazing smell of some of Julia's candles and soaps. It draws a lot of people into the café as well," Lisa pointed to the middle three shelves that were lined with Julia's products which she made by hand in the converted garage behind her house.

Lisa recognized the label as one that Simon was fond of buying and collected on his side of the bathroom sink. Kerry reached out and pulled a brown and gold bar from the top of the pile and raised it to her nose.

"What is this smell?" Kerry inhaled the warm scent she associated with Simon.

Lisa looked over the coffee grinding machine to see which bar Kerry was holding in her hand, "Oh, that's her Hemp and Patchouli bar. It is the most popular one. Julia comes in every second day to restock it. I think everyone in town has bought that at some point."

Kerry returned the bar to the pile and felt an uneasy feeling coil up in her gut.

Lisa was wiping the counter after she had scooped, ground, and bagged the beans for Kerry. A ritual they repeated every week, "Here you go."

There was no need for Lisa to tell Kerry the price since she already knew what it would be.

As Lisa counted out change from Kerry's twenty-dollar bill she looked up from her register, "Is everything okay?"

"Yeah. I was following a lead that I thought would help me with a case, but I hit a dead end," Kerry explained.

"The young girl?" Lisa asked.

Kerry knew it was a small town, but she was still surprised that Lisa knew.

"Were you up at the old Fox house?" Lisa asked, "I saw the cop cars there earlier."

Kerry nodded.

Lisa handed Kerry the change, "It's a shame about that house. It was beautiful. I remember when it went up in flames. Mrs. Fox watched in tears from the middle of the road. Her husband tried to get her to leave, but she refused to leave until the firefighters doused the last of the flames. Leaving only part of their home standing, and completely unlivable. They were devastated, but at least they had their lodge to move into after the fire took their home."

"What lodge?" Kerry asked as she slipped all the change from her hand into the tip jar.

"The Fox Lodge in Deception Bay?" Lisa said.

Kerry mumbled a quick thank you to Lisa as she ran from the coffee shop.

As she started her Jeep her heart pounded a little harder as she raced home.

She wasn't sure if Simon intended on coming home tonight, but she had to figure out a way to get out to Fox Lodge without him knowing, and she hoped the keys were still in his bag.

16

Fox Lodge was twenty minutes by boat and sat nestled in Deception Bay and was only accessible by water. After fifteen minutes of searching, Kerry found Simon's key for Fox Lodge in the back of the drawer of his night table. By the time Kerry located the key, Jim had left the marina for the day and her call went directly to his voice mail. Kerry was asleep by the time Simon returned home and she was able to slip out of bed and leave the house without waking him.

She waited until eight-thirty before she tried Jim again and this time, he picked up on the third ring.

"Jim speaking," his cheery voice rang through the line.

"Hi, Jim. I was wondering if I would be able to take the Grew out for a bit this afternoon?" Kerry asked.

"Changing your mind?" Jim asked.

"I just felt like taking it out for a bit of a drive today. The weather looks like it is going to be clear and I wanted to have a last trip on the lake before someone snaps it up," Kerry lied.

"Sure. It's your boat after all," Jim said. "Give me until two. It will take that long to unwrap it from storage and prep the motor."

Kerry thanked Jim and after she disconnected the call, she finished filling the report on Mr. Roberts and sent a personal letter of condolence to his daughter. Something she never did while working as a coroner in Montreal.

The buzz from Kerry's phone made her jump. She turned it over to see who was calling and then answered the call.

"Doctor Dearborne!" the technician on the other line spoke excitedly into the phone. "I wasn't sure how early I could call. But I didn't want to let it go too late into the morning. I know how interested you were in the additional test results."

"Slow down, Susan," Kerry prompted. "Take your time and tell me what you found."

"Well, as per your instructions I ran the tests you indicated on the blood samples you sent. Mostly I didn't find anything important. Your victim wasn't on any drugs, even prescriptions, and judging by the other indicators, she wasn't a drinker either. All her readings were within normal levels."

"So how is this news I can use Susan?" Kerry asked.

"Well, it was the last vial you sent with a note to sample any tests I could think of for a young woman of twenty-five to thirty who had been pregnant in the last year," Susan explained. "It was pretty vague, but it did give me some unique parameters to work within."

"Are you telling me you found something?" Kerry asked.

"Uh-huh," Susan teased. "I thought about the tests that would have been done on a pregnant woman. You know the more common tests that you know everyone would have, and I hit the jackpot when I focused on the victim's actual blood type."

"It was AB," Kerry said. "Nothing unusual about that."

"Not unusual but of concern when the blood type contains an Rh factor that is not compatible with the fetus."

Kerry's mind began to race ahead, predicting what Susan was going to say next.

"As you know, any mother who has an Rh incompatibility in their pregnancy will have to be given an immune globulin. When I checked the victim's blood for that, there were still traces in her blood."

"And there would be a record of any mother who was given an immune globulin during her pregnancy," Kerry added.

"That should be able to narrow down your search parameters," the young technician said.

"Great job Susan. You may just have found the link to how we can give our victim a name, and her family some answers."

"Oh, and I am also going to send you the report on the fibers of the clothes you sent into the lab. There were some traces of turpentine and oil on the victim's clothes. It will be in the email with the blood tests."

Susan emailed the official test results to Kerry once they finished their call. However, Kerry had already begun to draft an email that would go out to not only the hospitals she had flagged that were close to Lake Pines but all the hospitals in the country. With a more precise search of mothers receiving the specialized immune globulin, Kerry felt real promise that she would get a name for her victim.

The news of the blood results helped divert Kerry from the doubts and suspicions she had with Simon and Wayne. She decided to distract herself by focusing on the traces of turpentine and oil on the victim's clothes. That may help narrow down where she was held and hopefully lead her to the victim's killer. It made sense now that there weren't any animal tracks around the victim. The animals would have avoided the chemical smell in the ground.

Kerry made some notes about the findings in the test results then decided to head down to the marina a little early and see if Jim had her boat ready. But before she left, she opened her desk drawer and lifted out the folded piece of paper that contained the results from the soil tester. Kerry read the findings hoping to get a clue as to the contents of the ground where the victim was buried, however, as Kerry scanned the mineral count and toxins list, she noticed the sample from the site and the mud from Simon's boots matched. They both contained the same minerals and spores that were in the ground where the victim was buried, along with indications of turpentine and oil.

The marina was too close to drive to, and just far enough of a walk that Kerry was able to place a call to the police station. She decided to call Officer Jones, however, he had been called out to investigate an overnight break-in at the Hook & Anchor Bar. Kerry left her number with the receptionist, along with a short message that she was heading out to Fox Lodge to follow up on a lead.

The one thing Kerry learned from the beginning of her career is to not leave any reason for a judge to toss out a conviction because the correct protocols weren't followed. That's why after she spoke with the receptionist Kerry dialed Wayne's number to let him know where she was going. Kerry breathed a sigh of relief when her call went directly to his voice mail, where she could leave the appropriate information but not have to deal with Wayne wanting to tag along. Kerry wasn't sure she could disguise her distrust, and she didn't want to test it while out on an island.

When Kerry arrived, Jim had the Grew in the water and tied to a dock waiting for her.

Jim was standing on the marina porch speaking with a customer when Kerry arrived. She headed directly to her boat and turned to wave quickly at Jim as she walked along the dock.

Kerry untied the boat and quickly jumped in without looking up. She pushed the throttle into gear and turned the key. Once she was pulling away from the marina, she was able to relax a bit as she sat back for the duration of the ride. The entire way she wrestled a mix of emotions of what she wanted to find at Fox Lodge. Needing to find answers for her unnamed victim, but not wanting her suspicions to be confirmed.

As the boat neared Deception Bay, Kerry had an uneasy feeling that she was going to find the answers she needed there. And as she stepped off her boat and onto the dock, she couldn't shake the feeling she was being watched.

17

The lodge and its four outer buildings were set back from the water and surrounded by a forest of birch trees and brush. Time, and the predominant direction of the wind from the lake, had cut a path through the trees that allowed a current of air to flow toward the lodge. Kerry remembered the first time she stayed at Fox Lodge and the weekend she met Simon.

Among his other jobs as a hunting and fishing guide, Simon was a regular fixture at Fox Lodge. The owners took Simon on when he had finished high school and quickly realized that he was not only capable of taking care of the complete maintenance of the lodge, but he was also able to handle the responsibilities of the (sometimes difficult) guests.

The lodge was initially built to be used as a private hunting cabin, but the last owners had converted it into a commercial lodge to accommodate vacationers from around the country and the U.S. It was a few years later that additional sleeping cabins were added and they still dotted the property around the main lodge. Since then there has not been a summer that the reservations weren't solidly booked, however, the winter bookings had thinned out considerably.

The spring brought a familiar scent of mud and pine as the ground began to thaw on the island. The area around Deception Bay was popular among avid fishers because of the deep water and the consistent currents. There were few cottages this far out which also gave the guests at Fox Lodge the privacy and relaxation that they came to Lake Pines in search of.

The shoal–covered shoreline stretched from the waterline and folded under the grassy knoll where the canopy of birch began to thicken. The water lapped onto the rocks echoing their sound in the curved secluded bay where the private dock stretched into the bay. A mixture of moss and small wildflowers dotted the crevices of the rock and Kerry could see small buds revealing new growth.

The irony was not lost on her that she was investigating the murder of a young woman just as life was starting to bloom on the island.

She walked directly to the main lodge and quickly realized the key she held in her hand would be useless at getting into the cabin since the doors and windows were shuttered with large panels of wood that were custom-made to protect the cabin from the elements and animals. Except for walking around the exterior of the building, there was nothing she could see at the main lodge.

Kerry walked toward the four outer buildings. She wasn't surprised to also find the four cabins shuttered for the winter. Without a hammer or a crowbar, she was not going to gain access to the buildings. Kerry suddenly realized that like every resort, big or small, there was always a tool shed or maintenance area, and that is where she could find something to pry the doors open.

She found a small shed on the far side of the island which was hidden by a hedge of evergreen bushes. If it weren't for the slate rock path that was laid down in the ground, Kerry wouldn't have found the shed. She stepped on the uneven rocks, avoiding the muddy ground surrounding them, and came around a hedge of junipers.

Standing just under six feet high and four feet wide was an old stone shed with a slanted roof, no windows, and a thick wooden door. A wooden door that resembled the photo of the door sent to her by FGA Wood Products. The door was faded and worn with time. A low curve of mold coated the base of the door and reached up to the second hinge. Knicks and small gashes covered the door from where animals or intruders tried to remove the door from its frame.

Kerry pulled the keys from her pocket and tried each one in the single deadbolt until the door released from the latch. Kerry twisted the heavy steel handle and pulled the door open.

A wave of musty air exploded in her face and the stench of old dirt combined with engine oil was strong enough to taste. Kerry pulled the door wide and stepped inside. The light that filtered in through the door was the only thing that illuminated the inside of the stone shed. Except for the wretched stench that sank deep into her lungs, the small building was empty. The ground was loose beneath her feet and she could feel small stones roll beneath her shoes as she moved around inside the shed.

The inside of the door was pulled open and the sunlight shone on the door, and the scrapes and gouges were easy to see. They were recent enough that the color of the wood was lighter along the trail of scratches in the door. Kerry bent down and ran her fingers over the small gouges along the edge of the thick metal hinges and tears and anger rose inside her as she thought of the young girl who would have been trying in desperation to loosen the hinge from its frame. In her resolve to escape her capture, she never would have thought about the difficulty in trying to escape in that manner. She was just trying to get free. To get back to her child.

Kerry stood and turned around. There was no other way out of the shed. Kerry pulled out the phone from her pocket and flipped on the flashlight app in her phone and scanned it over the ground of the shed.

A dark, uneven stain covered a corner of the shed. The obscure discoloration permeated the stone where the young victim must have laid in her final moments after she was stabbed.

Kerry knew without formal tests or examinations that she had found the spot where the unidentified victim was held captive and was killed. She moved her phone around the ground in the shed and the light reflected off a small metal clip that lay nestled at the base of the stone wall. She reached down and picked up the clip with one of the plastic evidence bags she had tucked in her pocket.

With the clip safely in the bag, Kerry slipped it into her pocket.

No matter what she thought of Wayne, she needed to call him and have a site examination team sent out to the island before dark. Kerry stepped out of the shed, freeing herself from the stench and to where she could get cellular reception on her phone. She walked around the hedges and into the open field that led up to the main cabin and waited until the bars on her phone registered full reception.

When she was able to connect a call, she pressed Wayne's contact information and after a couple of rings, she could hear the faint crackle of Wayne's voice.

Kerry spoke loudly into the phone, "Hello Wayne? Wayne? Can you hear me?" Kerry walked closer to the water hoping the phone's reception would improve.

"Kerry I can barely hear you," Wayne answered.

"Wayne, I believe I found out where our victim was killed. I need you to get a team out here to collect some evidence from the shed," Kerry spoke quickly before her phone's reception weakened again.

"Where are you?" Wayne asked.

"I am at the Fox Lodge in Deception Bay. I'll explain more when you get here," Kerry was facing east as she spoke and as the sun shone behind her, a thin line from her shadow stretched over the rocks that lead down to the dock where her boat was tied. As she listened to Wayne ask for instructions, she noticed a second boat tied to the dock just behind her Grew.

Kerry took a deep breath and was just about to interrupt Wayne to let him know she was not alone on the island. But before she could speak a searing pain radiated from the back of her head and the light quickly faded from her eyes. As she collapsed to the ground there were only two things she would remember. The sound of Wayne's voice and the shape of the shadow that cascaded over hers.

18

The smell of smoldering ash made Kerry cough as she awoke in Wayne's arms. She was being carried out of the flames that were crawling up the forest of birch trees. Each tree looked like a match as it glowed in a cluster at the top, while their trunks stood charred. Wayne grunted and yelled for the others on the dock to help him as he stumbled across the grass until falling where the shoal rocks began to slope down toward the water. They both hit the ground with a thud and Wayne landed on

Kerry's left knee sending sharp shooting pain up her leg.

As she slowly regained consciousness, she began to cough up the smoke that had filled her lungs. Tears seared her eyes stung by the smolder that surrounded her as she lay on the ground.

Kerry couldn't tell how long she was unconscious, but the sky had darkened quite a bit since she was knocked out. She looked over at Wayne who was bent over on his knees and holding his body upright on his hands and he was frantically coughing trying to clear his lungs.

Suddenly, there were several people around lifting them both and trying to move them toward the dock. As Kerry was lifted that is when she noticed the shed, as well as the other buildings on the island, were engulfed in flames.

Firefighters worked three water pumps as they tried to contain the fire from the forest, no longer attempting to save the buildings. A loud cracking sound echoed over the forest as the thick beam that ran along the length of the main lodge collapsed under the heat flames and they all watched as a large plume of smoke and flames shot up into the air before it settled on the remaining section of the roof and then crawled down the timber siding.

Fox Lodge was gone. As was the shed that held the blood evidence that her victim was killed here. She kicked herself for not collecting some of the blood-stained dirt. She did, however, have the hair clip. She only hoped it would be enough to prove her theory that the victim was here. It would be Kerry's word against everything else. She should have come out with Officer Jones. Or Wayne, she thought, as she watched him try and regain his breath under the oxygen mask he held to his face.

Kerry leaned over and placed her hand on Wayne's arm, "Thank you, Wayne." She wanted to say something else, but the words wouldn't come. Except that a thick mass of tears choked them back as she tried to speak.

One of the firefighters wrapped a blanket over her shoulders, and he leaned over to examine the gash on the back of her head. Cool air struck her skin and stung where he parted her hair. He dabbed something cool over the cut and the applied pressure to the back of her head. Within a few minutes, he had a section of

Kerry's head bandaged and a bottle of electrolyte in her hand.

As Kerry gulped the blue liquid, she could sense Wayne was staring at her. She turned to face him and saw something she hadn't seen in him before. Concern. He was always working so hard to impress Kerry and the others he worked with that he never let himself seem vulnerable or at a loss.

"I am really glad you are okay," Wayne said.

"How did you know where to find me?" Kerry asked.

"The last thing you said before your phone went dead was that you were at Fox Lodge. Your voice sounded, well, funny. So, I came out to make sure you were okay. When I got here most of the island was on fire and it was by sheer luck that I found you." Wayne explained.

"I was knocked out on this hill. Where did you find me?" Kerry asked.

"Next to that small shed in the back of the island. I thought I heard some moaning and when I came around the corner, I could see your feet. When I went to drag you out all I could smell was gasoline," Wayne explained.

Suddenly the memory of the smell hit Kerry as well.

"I carried you out as far as I could and then I fell, like a clutz. How is your leg by the way?" he asked.

"It's okay. It's my head that is killing me."

Kerry and Wayne climbed into her Grew and one of the firefighters drove them back into town.

As the boat pulled away from Fox Lodge and out of Deception Bay, Kerry watched as the island burned. And she knew that it would burn throughout the night and that the smoldering ash and questions would be there when she awoke the next morning.

19

Kerry's head pounded and she tried to ignore the pain from where the nurse placed four stitches in the back of her head. Simon fussed over Kerry from the moment he came bursting through the doors of the emergency room bay where Kerry was lying face down while a nurse prepped the back of her head for the sutures. Kerry lay awake most of the night not because of the dull ache that throbbed in her head and knee, but from trying to sort out the events leading up to when Wayne pulled her from the fire.

She didn't want to get out of bed for the risk of waking Simon and sending him into a flurry of worry over her. Kerry drifted in and out of sleep but while she was awake her only thoughts lay with her victim, and she made a promise that she would find her family. Especially her baby. She wanted to give them closure so they could have a chance to move on.

After a breakfast of scrambled eggs, bacon, and coffee Kerry disappeared into the bathroom for a long hot shower. For a half-hour she let the hot water run onto her neck and over her shoulder slowly releasing the tension that built up over the night. She rubbed some menthol rub over her knee and the steam from the shower soothed her joint.

Once she assured Simon that she was feeling well enough to go into the office she left alone in her Jeep. She enjoyed being alone if even only for the short trip into her office. And she was still sorting out the questions she had about Simon. Maybe she would sleep at the office tonight. There was a cot in the backroom and tonight might be a good night to get it out.

Kerry parked along the curb and walked for ten minutes before getting her morning coffee at Joe Blacks. The air was still and warm and a light breeze rolled over her skin teasing at the first tastes of summer. A chill that hung in the morning air a week ago had finally disappeared and now the mornings were growing steadily warmer. Wildlife began to appear for glimpses in the park with their babies trailing behind. Another sure sign that the warmer weather was finally settling in for the season.

Kerry pushed open the door and waited for Lisa to turn around after the ding of the bell rang through the café. As expected, Lisa spun around to greet her customer. A smile crossed her face and she waved.

"I'll get your coffee for you, Kerry," Lisa busied herself behind the counter wiping the steamer nozzle before preparing the grounds of coffee in the press. Kerry glanced around the café and thought it seemed emptier than it usually did at this time in the morning. Her eyes stopped at the shelf of soap and she knew that any number of people in Lake Pines could have used that same soap. Kerry, herself, favored the lavender-scented ones. Simon couldn't have been the only one who used the one with patchouli one.

At the back of the café, a group of four people sat huddled at one of the small round tables. Kerry spotted Jim and Bernard who were sitting with two people Kerry did not recognize. Jim was too far away and too deep in conversation to even realize someone came into the café. The bell on the door was of no consequence to the four who were deep in conversation.

Kerry didn't want to field any more questions about the events of the night before and would just call Jim later to let him know she left the Grew tied up at his dock. They would deal with the particulars of selling the boat later. Kerry didn't want to think about that today.

Lisa was pouring the last of the foam on the top of Kerry's cup when Kerry turned her attention away from the table at the back of the room. Lisa reached for the cinnamon jar and sprinkled a light dusting over the top. She placed a lid over the steaming cup and handed it to Kerry.

"No charge today Kerry," Lisa smiled. "I know you had a hard night last night."

Of course, she did. Everyone in Lake Pines probably knew.

"Thanks, Lisa," Kerry turned to leave and as she reached for the door, she could feel the floor shake beneath her. The blast shook the building and tossed Kerry against the wall knocking her head against the corner of the counter. A high-pitched sound pierced her ears and her head spun in many directions. The hot coffee she was holding had landed on the floor and only a small amount splashed over her hand. She could feel the sting of the burn as her skin tightened from the pain of the hot liquid.

Stunned and dazed, the sounds in the room were muffled in her head. The crunching noise of stones and bricks falling around her as they settled on the floor of the café was the only distinguishable sound. The cracking of the glass from the oversized front window as each shard of glass fell from the metal frame. Some landing inside the café, the rest falling on the cement sidewalk outside.

A cry came from behind where Kerry landed on the floor. It was Lisa. She struggled to pull herself up, but her body felt weighed down. She looked around to see if something had fallen on her and prevented her from moving. Once she realized she wasn't trapped by some falling debris, she forced herself to her feet and fighting the throbbing pain and dizziness she looked around the rubble for any sign of Lisa.

She followed the sounds of her cries through the cloud of dust that hung in the air. She waved her hands in front of her face as she coughed out the dust that made its way into her lungs and she covered her mouth and called out Lisa's name.

Kerry found Lisa behind the counter with her leg pinned under a table that had flown through the air in the explosion.

Kerry dragged the table off Lisa's body and pulled her to her feet, "Can you walk?"

Lisa nodded, and together they hobbled out of the wreckage and rubble that five minutes earlier was a warm, cozy coffee shop. The smell of coffee was replaced with the distinct scent of dust and concrete.

On the street, onlookers began to gather, and arms reached out and grabbed hold of both Lisa and Kerry pulling them to safety. When they emerged from the cloud of dust that blew from the building, paramedics and firemen rushed toward the building.

"There are four people still inside," Kerry screamed at them. "They were sitting at a table at the back of the café."

Someone had flipped down the tailgate of their truck and Lisa and Kerry sat on it with blankets wrapped around their bodies and paramedics and police asking questions. Wayne came running from around the back of the building and went straight to where Kerry and Lisa were sitting.

"Are you okay?" Wayne asked. "What happened?"

Kerry just stared past Wayne and watched as the paramedics came out with the four bodies from the back of the café. Three were carried out in black zippered bags, and the last person was flat on a stretcher with an oxygen mask strapped to his face.

Kerry slid off the tailgate and pushed her way past the people on the street in front of her. As the body was lifted into the ambulance, she saw that the paramedic was holding Jim's familiar 'lakes are for fishing' hat.

There was a faint chirping of birds singing in the background and a pungent odor from the dust of the explosion as the sirens wailed, and Kerry watched as they loaded Jim into the back of the ambulance and drove away.

20

The staff at the Lake Pines Hospital weren't used to much more action than broken bones, cut lips, and the birth of babies often provided. In the last few hours, several scenarios that they wouldn't have predicted were tossed in their path. When Jim arrived at the hospital bay, three of the emergency room nurses burst out into tears and had to be replaced by a more senior nurse who was able to control her emotions. The team worked quickly to assess Jim and to stabilize his vitals. They weren't able to revive him, and he lay in a coma as the nurses tended to the cuts, scrapes, and burns he sustained during the explosion.

Kerry managed to convince the head nurse to let her sit by his bed and wait for him to wake up. She patiently waited, holding his hand as she spoke to him, hoping it would arouse him somehow.

She felt a light squeeze from Jim's hand, and she leaned in close to his face. His lips were moving but she couldn't hear what he was saying.

"I can't hear you, Jim," Kerry said. Hoping it would encourage him to try and speak louder.

"Get . . ." Jim muttered.

"Get what? Water?" Kerry reached for the glass on the table and bent the straw toward his mouth.

Jim closed his mouth and shook his head.

Then he tried again, struggling to get each word out, "Get. . .get. . .Wayne. . ." Jim muttered.

Kerry stared at him wondering what he meant and then once again he closed his eyes and she was unable to wake him.

She returned the glass to the night table and walked out from behind the curtain that circled Jim's bed. She found the nurse in charge and left her phone number.

"If there are any changes, or he says anything, please call me right away. Anytime."

Once Kerry was sure that the nurse understood the severity of the situation, she left the emergency room and walked out into the parking lot, and realized she didn't have her Jeep there.

She turned around intended to go back into the hospital to call a taxi when Officer Jones pulled up in a patrol car and stopped in front of her.

He lowered his window and shouted over to Kerry, "I need you to come with me to the station Doctor Dearborne."

Kerry ran to the passenger side of the car and yanked open the door and hopped inside.

"What's the matter?" Kerry asked.

Officer Jones threw the car into drive and pressed down on the accelerator, "We have arrested the person responsible for the explosion."

"That's great," Kerry said. "But why do you need me?"

"We also have arrested him for the fire at Fox Lodge," Officer Jones then looked at Kerry. "We also have reason to believe he is responsible for the murder."

Kerry sat back in the car seat, "That's great." Kerry didn't realize the police were so close to finding the murderer.

Officer Jones looked more upset than he should have for someone who just revealed the end of the town's nightmare.

"You should be happy," Kerry said.

"There's a problem though," he said.

"And what would that be?"

"We arrested Constable Burgess."

21

Kerry read the report three times and couldn't believe what she was seeing. She flipped through the pages and saw in print the evidence that was found against Constable Wayne Burgess. A few weeks ago, Kerry wouldn't have been surprised to read any of this, but since he pulled her from the fire, she was having second thoughts on the level of duplicity he was capable of.

She wasn't sure what surprised her more. The fact that there was such solid evidence against Wayne or that Officer

Jones had been investigating him for the last week and she didn't know.

"I didn't want to put you in an awkward position since you had to work so closely with Constable Burgess, with you being the coroner and all," Officer Jones explained.

"Don't you think that's exactly *why* I should have been told?" Kerry asked.

"I guess. Now that I look back. I just wanted to make sure since he is, or was, my supervising officer, that I followed all the correct procedures," Officer Jones said.

Kerry calmed the tone in her voice, "When did you first suspect him?"

"When I realized he gave you an altered hospital list. It seemed odd to me that he'd try and hinder your investigation in finding the name of the victim," Officer

Jones crossed his arms. "When I approached Mr. Wessex, he had doubts as well, but he wanted to remain impartial toward any inquiries, so he allowed me to investigate as long as it was in an undercover manner. That way if I was wrong then Constable Burgess' reputation wouldn't be harmed."

"The Mayor approved this?" Kerry asked.

"All undercover or covert investigations have to be approved by the council," Officer Jones explained. "It's a little-known bylaw that was enacted to fight corruption from within police stations in small towns."

"It says here in your report that Constable Burgess was seen coming from behind the café after the explosion. Who saw him?" Kerry asked.

"A citizen who wants to remain anonymous. At least for now," Officer Jones said.

"So, run through this for me again. How did you come to the point where you walked into his office and slapped cuffs on him?" Kerry asked.

"Well, as I said, I was suspicious after I realized the hospital list had been changed. But it wasn't until there was an eyewitness of Constable Burgess being behind the café that got the ball rolling in that direction," Officer Jones continued. "We pulled up the security video feed from the building behind the lane and, although it was blurry, we could see his figure tampering with the gas line behind Joe Blacks. That was enough to get a search warrant and when we went to

Constable Burgess' home, we found the evidence that is listed in that report."

Kerry read the list. Along with a hunting knife with a blade fitting the wound's description and dried blood stains, there were indications that Wayne also had planned the gas explosion at Joe Blacks. Buried in a storage cabinet in Wayne's garage, was a device like the one used to set the explosion on the gas line, along with a wrinkled pamphlet on how to construct a remote device. There was also a coat that smelled of gas believed to have been worn when the fire was set at Deception Bay, and finally, the missing portable music device and running shoes presumed to belong to the victim.

Kerry told Officer Jones that she was feeling a little lightheaded and wanted to head back to her office.

"I was thinking of calling in another coroner to handle the remainder of this case for you. And as well, to handle the autopsies from the three bodies from the explosion at Joe Blacks," Officer Jones said.

"And why would you do that?" Kerry snapped in anger at his suggestion.

"You are very close to this case, and I thought since you were part of the explosion you would want to remain impartial," Officer Jones explained.

"Are you implying that I may not be impartial?" Kerry asked, surprised and offended at his suggestion.

Officer Jones held up his hands and shook his head, "No Doctor Dearborne. I was just following the protocol that we were taught at the academy."

Kerry sighed and apologized for her outburst and thought maybe it would be better to continue their conversation after they both had time to let the news settle.

He offered to drive her to her Jeep, but she decided to walk and get some fresh air.

"It'll help clear my mind," she said.

When she arrived at her office she went directly to the fridge and filled a plastic evidence bag with ice and then rested it against the side of her head.

She tossed the printout of the arrest warrant on her desk and felt as if she had been hit in the gut. Not only was Wayne responsible for the murder, but he had also tried to kill her as well. She still didn't know who her victim was, but she was going to get hold of the pieces of evidence so she could have them examined herself.

Until then she had three bodies waiting for her in the examination room, already laid out on the stainless-steel tables waiting for autopsies. Although the autopsies would be a formality in these cases.

She began with Bernard Wessex, the town mayor. It was obvious when she initially unzipped the body bag that the cause of death was blunt force trauma that killed him. He was sitting at a table at the back of the café, against the wall, which was directly on the opposite side of the gas line where the explosion was set. The force of the explosion sent the bricks and metal from the back wall flying into Bernard's body at five hundred miles per hour. And judging by the distance he was sitting from the initial blast and the wall, and the damage he sustained, Kerry guessed he took the maximum force of the explosion.

Kerry moved over to the next body and unzipped the bag and extracted the zip lock bag that contained the victim's identification from the bottom of the table. His name was Jesse Dale and wasn't from Lake Pines but from Minnesota. He had a staff identification card for a chemical laboratory in Warroad. As with Bernard, Kerry determined Jesse also died of injuries sustained due to the blast of the explosion. Handing over Jesse Dale's body was going to require more paperwork since he was from the U.S. and Kerry had decided to stay late this evening and clear it off her desk. Especially with their town's police Constable being charged with the explosion, she wanted a smooth transition with his transfer.

The last victim was Ellison Hanover. Kerry had never met her but vaguely remembered seeing her around town. She had three kids and would often see her shopping with them when she was buying groceries or dropping them off at school when she was out for a run. She wasn't looking forward to seeing her husband or kids, but she knew she'd have to at some point to return her personal effects. Like her wedding ring.

Kerry completed the three examinations, returned each body to storage, and then sat down at her computer to prepare the official written statements.

She printed the three reports, slipped them in the appropriate envelopes, and then grabbed her coat and left her office. As she locked the door and headed toward the street, she decided instead of wondering why Wayne did what he did, she would ask him herself.

Kerry steadied herself as she sat in the cracked plastic chair and waited in front of the plexiglass shield that separated the prisoners from their visitors.

The large gray steel door opened into the room and Kerry watched from behind the glass shield as Wayne, looking tired and worn, was led out from the prisoner's holding area and into the visitor's room. He was dressed in an orange jumpsuit with the correctional facility logo stamped on the chest. The baggy jumpsuit did little to hide his slouched shoulders and dejected body language. The side of his face was beginning to show the signs of a bruise forming under a large red welt. A police officer being held with criminals would be a cop's worst nightmare.

And when he sat down and raised his face to hers, she realized she had never been this close to a killer before.

22

Initially, Kerry's instinct was to run from the room and avoid speaking with Wayne altogether. Then she thought of her victim. Her young unidentified victim lay in a cold box waiting to be named, and Kerry wanted her to be put to rest with respect and dignity.

"How could you Wayne?" Kerry blurted out, not exactly as she had planned to react.

"I didn't do it, Kerry," Wayne insisted. "I could never do something like that."

"There is some damning evidence against you Wayne," Kerry said. "I don't see how you can explain your way out of that."

Kerry held the page that had listed both the evidence against Wayne and a search on him that turned up a secret from his past that caused Kerry to cringe.

Wayne leaned in close to the small speaker in the base of the plexiglass partition, "I am being set up. It is the only explanation."

Kerry's face grew red with a mix of anger and disbelief and she tightened her grip on the paper, "Who would have set you up?"

"I don't know," Wayne said. Dejection and frustration present in his voice.

"I just want the victim's name, Wayne. Let me at least give her family that much. She has a baby," Kerry pleaded.

"I. Don't. Know." Wayne said, slamming his hand as he emphasized each word he spoke while fighting back tears. "I didn't do it."

Kerry lifted the paper from her lap and slammed it against the glass. Wayne stared at the printout and he shook his head as his eyes ran down the list of evidence against him. His eyes landed on the last item and his lips pressed together and he swallowed hard.

"I thought that record was sealed," Wayne said.

"Not from the police," Kerry said. "That's where I got the information from. Can you explain it?"

Wayne shook his head, "No. And I don't have to. It is irrelevant to all this false evidence against me."

Kerry pulled the sheet down and leaned in close and stared into Wayne's eyes, "Wayne, I just want to know who the girl is. Just give me a name."

Wayne looked right back at Kerry and without blinking he said, "I can't. I don't know who she is."

Kerry pushed back her chair and turned to leave the visitor's room, "Have it your way, Wayne. I'll find out, eventually."

Kerry pulled open the door that took her into the hall of the police station and away from Wayne's pleading face.

She knew he did it, now she had to focus on finding the identity of the victim and letting her rest in peace.

* * *

After leaving the police station there was only one person Kerry thought she could trust to give her any insight on what had happened over the last couple of weeks. She dialed Peter's number.

"Hello," Hearing his voice made her realize how much she missed working with him. His professionalism, skill, and kindness made even the toughest of cases easier to deal with.

"Peter, it's Kerry," Kerry sat on the bench in front of the museum. It faced the water and Jim's marina, which made her sad thinking of her friend who was in the hospital and in a coma right now fighting to stay alive.

"Hey, Kerry. What's up?" Peter said.

"I have no idea where to start," Kerry confessed.

"How about the beginning," Peter calmly suggested.

And that's what Kerry did. She explained everything to Peter from when she tripped on the victim's foot to her recent visit with Wayne. She even trusted her friend enough to reveal her concern with Simon and the problems they were having in their relationship because of her job offer from Jean.

Peter listened while Kerry explained her concerns on the case as well as her concerns in her personal life. Never once interrupting her as she spoke.

"Well, it sure seems as if you have had a lot on your mind," Peter said. "Let me start with your career dilemma, and you're not going to like what I have to say, but no one can make that decision but you. You must decide what you want to spend your week doing and where you want to do it. As for your serious concerns on this case, I may have some insight for you."

"Well, that's a start," Kerry said, grateful for any insight Peter could give her.

"I have worked with Wayne since he started in the department and, as you know, I even trained him. I would be the first to admit that sometimes Wayne can be, well let's say, less than attentive to detail. But it's not because he doesn't care, he gets nervous when he is working on an important case and when he is trying to impress a superior. I know for a fact that Wayne respects your skill and knowledge and I wouldn't doubt if he feels slightly inadequate when you are also investigating a case." Peter explained.

"That doesn't explain why he altered the information on the hospital list," Kerry said.

"His organization can be improved but I find it difficult to believe that he would have done that intentionally," Peter said.

"And what about his record? Did you know he had a police record when you took him on at the academy, and when you suggested him as your replacement?" Kerry asked.

Peter paused, "I thought those records were sealed."

"Well now that I know about them what am I supposed to think?" Kerry said.

"You could believe me when I tell you that it doesn't make a difference. It was a long time ago," Peter said.

"It was a charge of arson Peter! Don't you think it's a bit too much of a coincidence that Fox Lodge went up in flames?" Kerry asked.

"Yeah, I do," Peter said. "Look there is a lot you don't know about that charge. He didn't do it. Wayne took the fall for a few friends because he didn't want to rat them out. He was able to get his record sealed and only a sentence of probation because he shared information on a drug-smuggling ring that was going through Lake Pines. You can get the records from the courts. Most of the information will be redacted, but you'll get the gist of the information from what you will be able to see. You can make your mind up yourself, but you will be able to see the information regarding the arson."

Kerry spoke with Peter for a few minutes longer and then headed over to her office. She submitted a request to receive the court documents on Wayne's arrest and trial for the arson charge when he was a teen. Because of her position as the town coroner and Wayne's connection with the case she was working on, her request was approved and she received an email with the scanned document.

Kerry opened the file and as Peter said, most of the document was redacted. Important names and details of the drug smuggling ring were blacked out, as were some particulars surrounding the arson charge.

Some information was available such as Wayne's plea of guilty, his grandmother's agreement to vouch for Wayne on probation, and three names of the other suspected arsonists who Wayne refused to name. Of the three names two stood out above the others, Simon Phillips and Jim Chandler.

23

Simon's number flashed on Kerry's phone for the fifth time in the last hour. Finally, he gave up calling her and began to send a flurry of texts, none of which she responded to. Kerry felt more distant from Simon and was beginning to feel like she never really knew him. Even though Wayne was charged with murder, she still couldn't shake the questions she had about Simon and the tests she ran from the mud on his boots. It caused her memory to recall conversations that were out of the ordinary for her and Simon to have. Questions he asked about crime procedures and evidence she thought were just Simon showing an interest in her job, now held an ominous tone to his intention. She tried her best to find out more information regarding the charges against Wayne, but she soon realized that the information she received from the redacted document was the only information she was going to get.

Her phone buzzed again, and this time Kerry grabbed it and tossed it into her desk drawer so she wouldn't see the screen flash up Simon's photo every time he sent a text.

Kerry had paperwork she needed to complete on the autopsies of the three victims from the blast at the café and decided to distract herself with those. She had released the bodies to the appropriate funeral homes and had sealed the victim's belongings and prepared them for their return to their families. Kerry tried her best to clean the victim's personal items from the smoke and dust of the blast. All lasting reminders of how the three innocent victims died.

When Lake Pines Funeral Home picked up the last of the bodies, Kerry flopped down on the oversized chair in her office and closed her eyes. While she was working on the autopsies Kerry didn't want to think about the explosion. She was pushing aside her own traumatic experience of almost being killed and dragging Lisa out of the café, that she didn't give herself time to think about almost dying herself.

She was feeling guilty for not having gone to see Lisa and to make sure she was alright. Like Kerry she was banged up a little, but happy to have survived. An image of Jim flashed through her mind as she remembered him sitting in the back of the shop having a coffee, unaware of the explosion that would take the lives of his friends.

Kerry paused at that thought and then sat up straight. It was such an unusual mix of people. Amid the explosion and dealing with the aftermath, the glaring oddity of the group meeting for coffee at the back of the café never occurred to Kerry.

Until now.

She reached for the three files that sat on the table in front of her and flipped through each one, leaving each of them open to the page that contained their personal information. Kerry thought back to the museum opening and when Bernard had avoided Jim when he walked into the room. It was strange that they were together in a closed conversation when days earlier he didn't want to acknowledge him.

As a matter of fact, the more Kerry thought about the four sitting at the back of the café, no one at the table seemed to be reacting the way friends do when they meet for a coffee. She recalled their faces were serious and at moments their bodies were huddled together in tight conversation. The way you do when you don't want anyone around you to know what you are talking about.

Kerry pulled her phone out of her desk and retrieved Lisa's number from the police report.

"Lisa, it's me, Kerry," Kerry said into the phone the moment Lisa answered the line.

"Hi Kerry, how are you?" Lisa asked.

"I am sorry I haven't called sooner," Kerry said. "How are you feeling?"

"Pretty shaken up, but I am feeling grateful to be alive," Lisa paused, "I just feel so badly for the three who died and poor Jim is still in a coma I think."

"I know. It was pretty crazy," Lisa gave Kerry the perfect opening, "Hey, I didn't recognize two of the people with Jim. Do you know who they were?"

"No. I had never seen them in the café before. Except for Bernard, of course." Lisa answered.

Of course, Kerry thought. "Do you remember anyone out of the ordinary that may have been hanging around the café when you first arrived that day?"

"No," Lisa said. "Just like I told the police, it was just an ordinary day."

Except that we both almost got killed, Kerry silently thought, "If you need anything just give me a call. Okay, Lisa?"

No sooner had Kerry disconnected the line with Lisa when Simon's texts began to flash up once more. Kerry found it impossible to rest so she decided that leaving the building was the best choice.

She filed the reports away in her desk, grabbed her coat, and began to walk out of the door. Suddenly an email alert flashed on her phone. The medical records for a mother receiving the immune globulin came back with only one search result. Within the last year, there was only one young girl who had received the injections during her pregnancy.

And her name was Lia Bruce.

24

Kerry contemplated returning to the jail and forcing Wayne's confession by presenting him with the knowledge that she now knew who the victim was. She was determined to find the connection between Wayne Burgess and Lia Bruce. In retrospect, Kerry didn't know a lot about Wayne or his past. Everyone in Lake Pines had a similar story. They either were born and raised there or moved from somewhere else, and it didn't take long to figure out which camp a person was from. Kerry met Wayne when she first started dating Simon and before Wayne was hired at the police station. There was no reason to ask Wayne where he was from because it never took longer than twenty minutes for a conversation to veer toward a story from their past. A joke from a high school reunion or a laugh shared because of the memory of a camp mishap that one friend never let the other forget.

It wasn't an isolated trait to Wayne and Simon's friendship. Most people in Lake Pines had stories and memories that they jointly shared with other people in town.

Kerry was one of the few exceptions. She laughed alongside the others, but never really felt the camaraderie of the stories nor did she choose to share any from her past. Knowing they would all seem out of place.

Friends she made in Lake Pines never made her feel like an outsider, it was just a hazard of being a citizen of a small town when you were from somewhere else.

And as she walked out of her lab and caught the inquisitive glares that came her way, she remembered the hardest thing for her to get used to, however, was the lack of privacy in her day.

25

Lia Bruce. Now Kerry had a name for her victim, and she could start to search for her family to let them know what happened. No matter how horrible the news, Kerry learned from experience that it was worse on the families who didn't know what happened. The technicians at the police station had not been able to retrieve any of the owner's information from the portable music device that was among the other items of evidence found at Wayne's home. At least with a name, Officer Jones should be able to locate Lia's family. Kerry was eager to get news to Lia's family so they could begin to find closure and move forward.

Kerry called the station and the receptionist said Officer Jones was not in the office, but she expected him back soon. He got an emergency call and had to leave.

Kerry wanted to make sure she got the information directly to him and instead of leaving a message. She walked over to the station to wait for him and to tell him in person.

Kerry's phone buzzed as she was walking up the steps of the police station. At first, she didn't recognize the number, but then she remembered the first three digits of the nurse's station at the hospital were also 747.

"Hello, Doctor Dearborne speaking," Kerry answered.

"It's the nurse from Lake Pine's emergency room. You wanted me to call you if there were any developments with Mr. Chandler," as the nurse spoke, Kerry could hear the beeping of the machines behind her.

"Yes, I did. How is he?" Kerry stopped walking and turned around on the steps.

"He's awake now. He was asking for Constable Burgess but when I called the police station the receptionist said he was arrested!" The nurse said, shocked at the news.

"Yes, it's complicated. But it's fair to say he is not available," Kerry explained.

"That's when he said to call you," the nurse said. "He's awake and said he has something he will only tell you."

Kerry walked down the steps and quickened her pace as she ran toward her parked Jeep. She made it to the hospital and was running down the hall toward the emergency bay where Jim was being treated in less than twenty minutes from when the nurse had called her.

She whipped back the curtain and a nurse who was standing next to Jim's bed, switched off the monitor that recorded his vitals while the doctor was stretching a blue cotton hospital sheet over his face. Kerry's stomach dropped and the air in her lungs felt heavy. She was too late. Jim was gone.

Everything about Jim raced through her mind. He was one of the first true friends she encountered in Lake Pines and he was one of Simon's best friends.

"Oh, geez. Simon!" Kerry thought as tears flowed from her eyes. How was she going to tell him?

"Doctor Dearborne?" Kerry turned to face the voice that spoke to her. The emergency room nurse had placed a hand on her shoulder and handed her a tissue to wipe her eyes.

Kerry's body folded over, she grabbed her stomach and released the sadness that had built over the last week. She felt like she was going to be sick. The nurse rubbed her back and guided her to a row of seats at the back of the emergency room, next to a private bay. She pulled the curtain closed and sat beside Kerry until her crying subsided.

"I'm sorry," Kerry said. "It's just not fair. Jim was a great guy."

"I know. Everyone in town loved him. We're all having a really hard time with this," the nurse's eyes, lined red from crying. She held her shaking hand toward Kerry, "Um, he wanted me to give you this. He said to make sure you got this right away."

The nurse held out a folded sheet of paper and placed it in Kerry's hand, and folded her fingers shut.

"He told me what to write down and said I should only give it to you, and then swore me to secrecy. He said I should only trust you." The nurse leaned in close to Kerry, her lower lip trembling as she spoke.

The nurse left Kerry alone in the private bay while she read the note Jim dictated just before he died.

She wouldn't call it a confession, but Jim gave her the key she needed to find Lia Bruce's family. And her son. The important thing about the note was that Jim confirmed that Lia Bruce's death was not a random killing.

With the note tucked safely in her pocket she ran from the hospital. She knew the route by heart and that it would take an hour to get there. But before she left town, she needed to grab something from her office and make a call.

With her left hand on the steering wheel, she dialed the number with her right hand. The phone rang once before he answered.

"Simon, it's me, Kerry. I need your help."

26

Simon held the redacted sheet in his hands and was able to read past the blacked-out lines. His memory found it hard to erase that point in his life and the horrible week he spent standing in the back of the courtroom. It was at that point in his life that he made a crucial decision. Either he continued the path he was on and ended up in prison, or he started to suck up some responsibility and get his life in order. He worked hard and chose the second option. For years Simon worked hard to build a reputation as an honest hard worker. Geraldine Fox was Simon's high school teacher and believed he was a good kid at heart. She offered to give him a second chance, and his first real job. On one condition. That he never gets mixed up in any drugs or with any gangs. No matter what.

Simon eagerly agreed to regular drug tests and he also volunteered at Holy Rosary every Sunday after mass serving coffee and sweets to seniors. Simon found it tough to follow rules set by someone else, but he was immensely grateful for the opportunity and the chance for a clean start that he swallowed his pride. Wayne had been saved from the clutches of jail by Constable George, and together they promised to put this bad moment in their lives behind them and to keep each other from making the same mistake again.

Their friendship stretched a lifetime, but it was the secret between them that held them together.

Simon turned the sheet over on his lap, "I'm sorry I never told you, Kerry."

Kerry didn't turn her face from the road in front of her. She still didn't know how to feel comfortable in such a closed area with Simon, "How come you never told me?"

"I don't know," Simon said, then corrected himself. "Actually, I do know. I was afraid you wouldn't want to be with me. I didn't think you would think I was good enough for you if you knew."

"That's why you are so protective of Wayne, isn't it?" Kerry asked. Their close friendship made more sense now that she knew about what happened to them as teens.

Simon nodded.

"I had been trying to call you all morning. And I sent you texts too," Simon said.

"I know. I needed to figure some things out first," Kerry explained.

"Is that why you called me? Did you figure things out?" Simon asked, the shyness noticeable in his voice.

"Not completely," Kerry handed Simon the note Jim dictated to the emergency room nurse before he died. "I called you because of what Jim said in that note. Among other things, he said I needed to trust you and that you can fill in the blanks where Wayne is concerned."

Simon wiped the tears from his eyes and he began to reveal the entire story to Kerry.

"It began when we were about sixteen. Wow, that seems so long ago," Simon looked out at the lake as they drove along the highway. "A bunch of us would often get together and go on day-long boat trips in the summer. Sometimes we would end up at beaches and go for a swim. Other times we would cliff jump, or just float around. One day, when it was particularly nice, we just kept driving. It wasn't until we stopped that we realized we ended up in Warroad, Minnesota. We laughed at the idea that we made it all the way down without getting stopped by the border guards. That's when Wayne joked that we could make a fortune by driving down some beer and cigarettes to some of the residents. At that time, the selection of beer was better up here." Simon chuckled as he recalled the summer from his past.

"Anyway, not before too long, we had a bit of a drink run going. A guy from Warroad approached us and offered to give us a thousand dollars to get a box up to a friend who lived close to Lake Pines. We didn't know it at the time, but we were transporting drugs. It was stupid, but we didn't ask any questions because the money was too good. When we realized what was happening, we tried to get out of it. That's when Wayne was framed for setting fire to an old cottage on the lake. An undercover operation of the provincial police force had been trailing us and gave Wayne a choice. Go to prison or give up everyone involved."

"And that was the court record I saw," Kerry said.

"Wayne didn't want to give up me or any of our friends, so he took the wrap for the fire. Constable George stepped in and vouched for Wayne and brokered a plea deal for him. In return for the name of our connection in the U.S., Wayne received probation instead of jail time, and our names would be kept out of any trial. And that's it."

Kerry relaxed her grip on the steering wheel, "I wish you had told me, Simon."

"And how would you have reacted?" Simon asked.

Kerry let out a sigh, "Probably not great. I'm sorry."

"That's okay," Simon continued to stare out the window, wiping tears that ran from his eyes. Not only was a best friend of his now dead, but another was also sitting in a jail cell for crimes that Simon was positive he didn't commit.

"So how is Jim caught up in all this? He doesn't seem like he is the type to be involved with killers?" Kerry asked Simon.

"He's not," Simon rubbed the side of his head. "Although he never admitted it, I think he was still mixed up with that guy in the U.S. and getting stuff in and out of Warroad. Money never seemed to be a problem, and even when the cottage business died off, his marina never seemed to take a hit."

"But he obviously knew who the victim was all this time and never said anything," Kerry said. "And how else would he have known where her son is? And why tell me now?"

Simon was as perplexed as Kerry was and had no idea how to respond.

Kerry pressed her left turn indicator and eased onto the dirt road that would carry them for another half mile to a small isolated cabin. Smoke rose from the slender chimney that pierced from the cedar-shingled roof. Toys lay strewn on the covered porch that ran the width of the log cabin. Two large wicker chairs were angled toward each other on one end, and a large red flowerpot ready to be planted with fresh spring flowers stood bare on the other.

Kerry parked her Jeep and waited at the end of the driveway. She turned the engine off and unclipped her seat belt.

"Is this the address where Lia Bruce lived?" Simon asked.

"Maybe. This is the address Jim said we can find Lia's baby. It may be her parents' house. Either way, I thought it would be better to come out in person to tell them their daughter died. Not the kind of news you want to tell someone over the phone," Kerry hesitated as she sat in the driver's seat.

"What's wrong?" Simon asked.

"I was just thinking. This moment will change her son's life forever, and he will never even remember it."

The Jeep sat in the driveway long enough for the woman in the cabin to notice. After peering out the front window she opened the front door and stepped onto the porch. She held a hand over her eyes, shielding them from the sun, and waved to Kerry and Simon sitting in the Jeep.

"She seems kind of young to be Lia's mother," Kerry said.

"That's because she's not her mother," Simon suddenly realized why Jim said in his note that he wanted Kerry to bring him along when she came out here. "That's Patricia Jones."

Kerry looked at Simon, "Who?"

"Officer Clayton Jones sister!"

27

Patricia was twelve years younger than Clayton and the only child of their father's second marriage. Clayton had been very protective of Patricia from the time she was born. When their father wasn't drinking, he was knee-deep in an argument with anyone within striking distance. His children included. Which left Clayton and Patricia at the mercy of Patricia's mother. The source of her anger and random outbursts was a mystery to Clayton and Patricia when they were growing up. It wasn't until the day before

Patricia's tenth birthday when her mother left the house to pick up her birthday cake and never returned that they began to realize it had little to do with them, and more to do with Clayton Senior. Later, Patricia found her birthday card tucked under her pillow along with a note saying she couldn't stay in an abusive relationship any longer and that she would be back to get her and taker her away. The years passed and Patricia's mother never returned, and soon Patricia stopped waiting.

Clayton had already played the role of a parent to Patricia for most of her life, so when he approached the court to be her legal guardian, nobody was surprised, and it just became a matter of formality. Simon told Kerry that while growing up, every guy in Lake Pines knew that Patricia was off-limits. No matter how much a guy liked her or wanted to ask her out, the fear of having to deal with Clayton was enough to scare them away.

Now Simon was sitting at Patricia's eight-foot-long harvest table with Kerry trying to come up with a reason for their sudden visit. Before they got out of the Jeep, Kerry told Simon she didn't want him to alert Patricia to the real reason they were there. If Lia Bruce's baby is here, then that means Patricia, and possibly Clayton could be connected to her murder. They devised a plan that they'd hope would work.

"So how did you find out that I did flower arranging Simon?" Patricia placed three mugs on the table along with cream, sugar, and spoons while the coffee was brewing.

"I heard it somewhere in town, not sure from who," Simon fidgeted with his phone in his pocket.

"Well, it is just something I started not long ago. Clayton thought I would be good at it so I thought I would give it a try," Patricia pulled the carafe out of the coffee pot machine and carried it to the table, and filled the mugs.

"We were thinking of something small and private," Kerry interjected. "So just a simple arrangement would be good. We just wanted to get some ideas before we make a decision."

"Wow, Simon. I never thought you were the marrying type," Patricia chided, but secretly, she wished that Simon had asked her out when they were younger. She wished anyone would ask her out at this point. She was starting to think she was going to die out here alone in this cabin.

"Well, people can change I guess," Simon said. He reached for the small white jug and filled the remaining space in his mug with the cream.

The kitchen was situated at the back of the house and looked down from the top of a hill that cascaded toward a small pond. A slim finger dock extended from the manicured lawn that was lined with flower boxes and miniature windmills. In the center of the pond was a floating dock that swayed with the breeze but never drifting too far from its anchored position.

A canoe and two kayaks were flipped over on the crescent-shaped beach that was strewn with colorful children's toys next to the water's edge.

The kitchen flowed seamlessly into the family room area that boasted an oversized stone fireplace and a collection of expensive furniture pieces that were all upholstered with matching tan leather material. The back of the house was a continuous wall of floor-to-ceiling windows that were designed to accommodate the sunlight that poured in no matter the angle of the sun or the time of year. Above the fireplace hung a painting that struck Kerry as out of place and held her attention long enough that Patricia noticed her staring.

"Isn't it beautiful?" Patricia said.

Kerry nodded, "Very. Where did you get it, I've been looking for some new artwork for my place?"

"Clayton bought it for me for my birthday last year," Patricia said. "He said he got it at that little gallery in Lake Pines."

The cry of a baby echoed from the far end of the hall and reverberated under the ten-foot-high ceilings in the cabin. Simon snapped his head toward Kerry. She caught his movement out of the corner of her eye, but with Patricia watching her, she didn't want to seem fazed by the sound.

"Oh geez, the little guy is up," Patricia pushed back her chair and excused herself as she ran down the hall and into a room where the crying baby was.

"That must be him," Simon whispered. "What do we do?"

"Nothing yet," Kerry said. "There's something off about this place," Kerry whispered.

"Yeah, it's freaking gorgeous," Simon said.

"A little too nice," Kerry nodded her head toward the fireplace, "That painting is worth a fortune and there's no way Clayton got that at the gallery in town."

"How do you know?" Simon asked, still in a whisper.

"That's a Lawren Harris painting," Kerry said. "And Mrs. Kerr only sells those kitschy paintings done by locals. Not million-dollar Group of Seven paintings. I'd hazard a guess that Patricia has no idea what is hanging above her mantelpiece."

Kerry could hear footsteps in the hall.

"When I give you the signal, I want you to distract Patricia."

"What signal?" Simon said.

Patricia walked back into the main room of the cabin and across from Kerry and Simon at the harvest table. "I'm sorry about that. This little guy must be going through a growth spurt, he's always up to eat every few hours." Patricia giggled as she wiggled her fingers under the baby's chin until he began to smile and coo at her. She grabbed a bottle from the fridge and ran it under warm water from the tap at the kitchen sink. A little while later she was walking back to the table balancing the baby on her right hip and the warm bottle in her left hand.

"So, do you have a color theme you were leaning toward," Patricia rested her left foot on her right knee and nestled the baby against her leg, and popped the warmed bottle in his mouth.

Kerry reached for the coffee mug, intentionally knocking over the creamer, sending the thick white liquid across the table and spilling toward Patricia.

Just as Kerry had hoped, Patricia jumped up to get a cloth.

"Here, let me hold the little guy," Kerry offered with outstretched arms.

Patricia didn't hesitate as she thrust the child into Kerry's arms and then turned and ran to the cupboard and grabbed a handful of tea towels. She dabbed at the spilled cream and Simon started to collect the mugs and spoons where the liquid was pooling beneath them on the table.

Kerry stood up with the baby and walked toward the wall of windows and pretended to be soothing the youngster as she withdrew the blood sample device from her pocket. She placed it under the baby's foot and pressed it against his skin. As she did so, a minuscule needle ejected from the case in less time than it would take to blink. She was distracting the baby enough that he didn't scream, but it was enough time to get the sample she needed to confirm if this was in fact Lia Bruce's child.

She slipped the device back into her pocket just as Patricia was coming over to collect the baby.

"Sorry about that," Patricia grabbed hold of the baby and kissed the top of his head.

"He is a real sweetie your son," Kerry said as she handed the baby back to Patricia.

"Oh, he's not mine," The baby began to fuss, and Patricia wiggled the bottle nipple against his cheek until he grabbed hold and began to suck. "My brother asked me to watch him because his mother took off on him a little while ago. He works for the police station and was on duty when the baby was brought in. They were about to call social services and he didn't want him to go into a strange home so he arranged to have me approved to watch him until they can find a proper foster home or adoptive parents."

"That's hard to imagine," Kerry said.

Patricia agreed, "I don't think I could ever give him up now."

Kerry excused herself and asked to use the bathroom. Once she disappeared into the third room down the hall, she checked the results of the blood test.

She closed the door to the bathroom and pulled out the testing device. It was one that she had specially ordered and used on difficult cases when in remote locations, such as those around Lake Pines. It was useful in obtaining over thirty quick blood sample results in less than two minutes. The problem with the machine was it had to be used on either a living person or a recently deceased victim which meant she couldn't use it for most of her cases. When she ordered it, the machine used up three-quarters of her annual budget, but she thought it would be well worth the investment. As it blinked the results, she knew that even if this was the final time she ever used the device it would've been worth all the flack she received from the provincial health minister for buying it without his approval.

Kerry turned on the water tap and pulled out her phone and called the one person she could trust and that she knew could help her.

"Hi, Peter. It's Kerry. I have a name for my victim, and I don't think it was a random attack. I think her murder was intentional. Her name is Lia Bruce and I was also right about her having a baby in the last year as well. Look, I'll explain it all in more detail later but I found her baby and I need your help. There is a bit of a twist to the case now and I need you to trust me," Kerry spoke softly into her phone.

"Why not call Officer Jones? He's in charge now," Peter said.

"That's the twist," and Kerry gave Peter a summary of the situation and he understood why she could only call him. Once she was off the phone, she shared the location of the cabin from the maps device on her phone and slipped it back into her pocket.

She turned off the water tap and walked out into the main area of the cabin where she would wait for Peter to arrive with his own team of police officers.

28

As Kerry suspected, Peter arrived completely prepared. His team pulled up to the cabin without sirens blaring or lights flashing. He texted Kerry from the dirt road moments before he was about to pull into the driveway, and parked alongside Kerry's Jeep and the forensics team parked their van behind his car. Peter walked toward the cabin with a middle-aged woman with long dark hair and a warm calming smile. The social worker Peter called was a seasoned professional that brought with her an emergency child protection certificate, all her credentials, and a warm disposition. When Kerry received Peter's text, she stood without a word, walked to the front door, and opened it just as he was stepping onto the porch.

Jenna Patchett was the kind of woman who spoke as gently as she walked. Her soothing voice was either a trained attribute or a fortunate natural trait that she no doubt found useful when approaching emotionally charged situations that involved distraught children and family members. Her soft eyes conveyed sympathy without judgment and she was able to read the tension in the room and disarm Patricia's rage when she reached out to take the baby.

Patricia's perplexed reaction to seeing Peter and four officers walk into her cabin proved to Kerry that she had no knowledge of the circumstances that surrounded the small child that she held in her arms. Nevertheless, Patricia sobbed as an officer recited her rights and told her she was being charged on suspicion of kidnapping and murder. Kerry could hear her protests as she was taken from her home and placed in the back of one of the awaiting police cars that were parked at the end of her driveway.

She yelled through her tears to call her brother and that he'd sort everything out. He was a police officer, after all. Surely, that should count for something!?

Kerry rubbed her hand over the child's head as Jenna cradled him in her arms. His head tucked securely in the nape of her neck as she hummed a gentle tune. It was easy to see how Jenna found her profession of social work, and why Peter thought she was the right person to bring along.

Peter pulled Kerry aside and told her he had obtained the authority to take over the murder case of Lia Bruce considering that Wayne Burgess was being held in the Lake Pines jail and the murder victim's child was found at Clayton Jones' house with his sister.

"I've also requested an arrest warrant for Clayton, and it is going to be sent to me within the next half hour. I'm just waiting for the judge to sign it," Peter put his hand on Kerry's shoulder. "You did a great job, Kerry. But I'm glad you felt you could call me."

Kerry smiled, "I miss working with you, Peter. This case is just one example of how messed up things are in Lake Pines."

Simon walked over to where Kerry and Peter were standing, "Look, I hate to interrupt you both, but I think it would be fair if we revisited the charges against Wayne. Don't you think?"

This time Simon was speaking to Peter.

"I don't disagree," Peter said. "I was just telling Kerry that I am going to be heading up this case from this point on. As soon as I take Clayton into custody I want to sit down and review all the paperwork on this case. And from the little bit of summary I did get from Kerry, there is a heck of a lot to go through."

Kerry and Peter agreed to meet up in town later at her office and come up with a plan on how to proceed.

"I think right now the priority needs to be how to find Lia's family. There's someone out there who is missing her and that little baby. We need to get him home," Kerry said. "And soon."

"I'm already on that. I have one of my officers tracking down all contact information on anyone with the name Lia Bruce, and I'm sure I'll hear something soon. He's the best in my office," Peter said. "I know how important this is."

Kerry and Simon drove back to Lake Pines along the same single-lane highway, but this time Kerry asked Simon to drive. She was feeling drained from the emotions that ran through her over the last few days. It still hadn't fully sunk in that Jim was dead and that Clayton had something to do with Lia's murder.

Kerry also had to face the fact that at one point in her investigation she even suspected Simon may have had something to do with this case. She had to reconcile her feelings and why it was so easy to think the worst of the man she loved. She knew the only way she could do that was to come clean with Simon and tell him everything she was feeling during the investigation and maybe, somehow, they could come out the other end. Hopefully closer, or at least as healthier friends.

Kerry spoke for twenty minutes without Simon interrupting. He listened as she laid out the evidence that led her to believe the worst in him. She wasn't even sure if it was what pushed her away or if she just found it easy to see him in a negative light.

"It was everything Simon. You being out of town and the right moments, the hunting knife, the same mud as Tunnel Island on your boots and even the incident at Fox Lodge," Kerry listed off each item and realized how easy it would have been for someone to point evidence like that so easily toward Simon. And even to frame Wayne. Especially if it was Clayton.

Simon relaxed his shoulders, "I can see why you were reluctant to talk about Montreal. Especially, if you thought I could've been involved."

Kerry spoke up quickly, "But never with Lia's murder, Simon. I never could get to the place where I thought you could have murdered someone. I'm just so sorry."

Simon reached out and placed his right hand on top of Kerry's. He slipped his fingers through hers and lifted her hand to his face. He leaned over and placed a soft kiss on her hand and then lowered their hands to her lap.

They drove in silence the rest of the distance to Lake Pines. Falling in love with Simon almost two years ago was the easy part, admitting to herself that she could have judged him so incorrectly was the hard part. As they drove closer to Lake Pines Kerry was starting to feel like she did soon after she first met him, and that things were going to be easy with Simon again.

29

Simon parked Kerry's Jeep in front of the police station and turned off the ignition. They sat parked for a few moments, both staring out the front of the Jeep's window and hesitating to look at each other. A lot had unfolded throughout the day and both were feeling unsure as to what to say.

Ultimately, it was Simon who made the first move. He reached out and grabbed hold of Kerry's hand and gave it a gentle but firm squeeze.

"You know I love you, Kerry. Don't you?" Simon asked.

"I know you do Simon," Kerry said. "But there are some things we need to speak about and sort out if we are going to be able to move forward together."

"There are some things I need to tell you," Simon admitted. Kerry's mind flashed back to the diner and the woman he was eating with. "But maybe it can wait until we sort out everything here."

They were parked outside the police station where Wayne was being held since the afternoon he was arrested for Lia Bruce's murder.

Simon and Kerry had agreed when they turned onto Main Street that it was more than a slim possibility that Wayne was innocent and at the very least, he deserved to be heard again. Simon didn't have to work too hard to convince Kerry to give Wayne some time to explain himself, and together they walked up the police station steps holding each other's hand and feeling more like a team than they ever had before.

Kerry smiled as she approached the officer on duty who oversaw registering all visitation for anyone being held in their cells.

"I'd like to visit with Constable Burgess please," Kerry said. "You can tell him that Simon Phillips is also here."

Kerry wasn't sure if Wayne would have agreed to see her if he thought she was here on her own. However, having Simon present would ensure his agreement to meet.

"I am sorry Doctor Dearborne," the officer said. "He's been transferred to the holding cell at the courthouse."

"Why is that?" Kerry asked. It seemed late in the day to transfer anyone to the court. Especially with everything so close in Lake Pines.

"Because his trial has been moved up to tomorrow morning, and there is a hearing for his bail tonight," the officer folded his hand over his desk. "I'm sorry you wasted your evening."

Kerry glanced at Simon, and he also looked confused about Wayne's transfer. Knowing there was little she could do at the police station, Kerry stepped away from the counter and turned to leave, and thanked the officer.

"Okay, thanks," Kerry raised a short wave to the officer and turned toward the exit. She had her right hand on the door and then abruptly returned to the admission desk.

She had an uneasy feeling strike her gut. "Who did you say authorized the transfer?" Kerry asked.

"I didn't," the officer joked.

Kerry tilted her head and the officer shot Simon a sideways joking smile and mumbled, "The coroners never get my sense of humor."

The officer opened his logbook and ran his finger down to the last entry, "It was Officer Jones."

"When did he leave?" Kerry asked.

"About ten minutes ago," the officer said.

Kerry ran from the building and took the steps two at a time. Simon was already ahead of her and opening the driver's side of the Jeep and had the ignition started before she climbed in.

As Simon drove toward the courthouse, Kerry had a strange feeling Wayne wasn't going to be there.

30

Every time Simon stepped inside the courthouse a shiver ran up his spine. It reminded him of how close he came to making the wrong choices in his life. The decisions he made the summer Wayne was arrested, would have surely earned him a police record and fewer options in his life. Kerry would probably not even given him a second glance and the incredible opportunity in front of him right now wouldn't exist.

He knew he had to get used to being here, and he had to remind himself that he did nothing illegal. The only thing he had left to face were the lies he had been telling Kerry over the last year.

Kerry walked toward the court clerk and offered her best professional approach and smile that she could muster under the circumstances. She knew that looking flustered and rushed would only raise the ire of anyone she was looking to get information from.

As it turned out, the clerk on duty was not easily swayed, and almost seem to have an affinity for keeping a pleasant demeanor hidden.

Kerry placed her identification card on the counter and briefly explained the change in the chain of command in the recent investigation into the murder victim found on Tunnel Island.

"Constable George is now in charge of the investigation. If you contact him I'm sure he'll assure you that I am permitted to all the information on Wayne Burgess," Kerry knew that everyone in the judicial system in Lake Pines was familiar with Peter and she recognized over time that he didn't have one person in town that was unwilling to help him.

"I don't know who told you there was a hearing tonight," the nasally court clerk sat behind her desk and methodically tapped her index finger on the counter as she spoke. "How many times do I have to tell you?"

"Please, it's very important," Kerry pleaded. "Can you check again?"

"I don't have to," the clerk leaned over her desk and spoke louder than she had before. "The Judge won't be back until

Tuesday, and when he does return his docket full with people arguing their traffic violations."

Simon pulled Kerry away from the clerk's desk aware that not only were they not going to get any information from the clerk, "You know what this means, don't you?"

"That Wayne isn't here, and he could be in danger," Kerry said, reading Simon's thoughts.

Simon ran his fingers through his hair, the way he always did when he was upset, "We have to find him, Kerry. If Clayton is responsible for killing Lia and burying her on Tunnel Island, Wayne doesn't stand a chance."

"He wouldn't have taken Wayne to his house. Not with Patricia and the baby there," Kerry said. "There must be some idea of where he would have gone. If Clayton wanted to disappear with Wayne and not be found, he'd probably go to a location he knew quite well. Maybe somewhere his family used to go, or where he went with friends a long time ago. Perhaps even where he would have gone on a vacation once."

"You're right," Simon agreed.

"He'd have had to take Wayne somewhere private. Somewhere that no one would know about," Kerry said.

Simon stopped running his hand through his hair, "I got it!"

Kerry was about to ask Simon what he was talking about when he suddenly broke into a dash and headed out into the parking lot.

Kerry ran after Simon, catching up to him just as he was putting the Jeep into drive.

"Are you going to tell me what you're doing?" Kerry asked as she climbed inside.

"I know where Clayton took Wayne. And we need to get there soon or we won't have a chance to save him."

Simon sped out of the parking lot and headed down Main Street and both he and Kerry hoped it wasn't too late.

31

Kerry's boat was tied up to the dock and they found the key under the passenger seat where Jim left it for all his customers. After a quick turn of the key, the engine revved to life. Simon threw the throttle down and shot out of the slip sending a cascading wave of water over the dock. Kerry could hear the other boats hitting against each other and the wooden slats on the dock when the wake of the Grew hit their hulls. Simon hadn't been to Clayton's cottage for years but like most cottages on the lake, he remembered where it was.

Clayton was an awkward kid growing up. Simon only remembered being at his house once when they were small, and the recollection of Clayton's father passed out on the couch stuck in his mind. Mostly, because there were several empty beer cans on the floor and an empty bottle of whiskey turned over on its side and resting against the table. Although Simon never said anything, he knew Clayton was embarrassed, and because of that, Simon was never invited back. The summer Simon was at Clayton's cottage was the summer they turned fifteen. Clayton invited a bunch of guys out for a big camping week in the middle of July when his father was away on a fishing trip. The air was heavy with the humidity the heatwave of the summer brought, making the air feel heavy even after sunset. Simon had brought a tent but because of the extreme heat, he didn't bother to set it up. Instead, he chose to sleep on the deck of the old boathouse that hung over the water in the bay.

Simon thought the breeze off the water would keep him cool as he slept.

The boathouse was built on stilts to accommodate the frequently changing water levels in the bay. Deception Bay was situated near the water dam and depending on the flood forecast of the season, the water could either be low or high. After years of replacing boards and dock cribs, Clayton Senior decided to build it high enough to accommodate the highest water level.

This, unfortunately, made it impossible to access during regular or low seasons, which is what happened most summers. A second dock needed to be built on the far side of the bay for boats to tie up at, and to make it easy for passengers to disembark.

The error in the building design of the boathouse inadvertently created the perfect location for parties. When they'd hang out at Clayton's cottage during the summer, the raised elevation gave the boys the perfect vantage point to see parents before they reached the island. A few minutes was all they needed to clear the room, but the outlandish boathouse design gave them fifteen to remove any bottles.

Another feature that gave Deception Bay its name was the uncommonly deep water and strong water currents. Even during summers with low water levels, Deception Bay took the lives of many weak swimmers who kayaked or swam out a little too far and couldn't make it back. The strong current along with the deep water and submerged caves made finding bodies of drowned swimmers almost impossible. It was how it got its name.

It was during one summer that Simon saw something he was never able to forget.

There were five of them set up in the boathouse. They were on their third beer of the evening and they began to play some drinking games to pass the time. They were all too old and grown-up for board games, and too young to sit around and discuss their lives. Simon remembered starting off the group with a series of truth and dare questions. It didn't take long for the boys to become disinterested in that game. Since they were all friends from the moment they were born and knew all there was to know about each other, the game turned out to be a flop. There was little incentive to take the dare option, which usually proved more fun during a game such as that.

Clayton suggested a game called 'would you rather'.

The idea was for them each to take a turn and to present someone with the choice between two options. Hopefully, being inventive enough that both options proved to be cringe-worthy.

On Clayton's second turn he chose Gilbert and asked him if he'd rather swim out to the floating buoy off the island in the dark or stay locked in the boathouse closet for ten minutes.

Gilbert, not a strong swimmer or a fan of dark water, chose the ten minutes in the closet.

The closet was only a few feet away from where the group sat drinking on the boathouse deck but to anyone who didn't know it was there, it would have been completely hidden among the wall of panels. The door was disguised well enough that none of the boys knew it even existed until that night.

Gilbert followed Clayton to the back of the room next to the deck and waited while Clayton removed a small piece of trim and slid his hand into a groove just large enough for three fingers to fit inside. The boys watched as Clayton pulled open the panel, and as if they were watching a scene out of a spy movie, they gasped in unison.

The first impression was how cool it would be to have a room like that. None of them would have been able to say why, just that it would have been neat.

Once the panel was open, Clayton stepped to the side and allowed Gilbert to walk into the closet. The area was small, maybe only four feet by three feet, and was shrouded in complete darkness. There was no window to the outside nor was there a light wired into the space. The boys watched as Clayton closed the panel and replaced the trim to the edge, sealing it from sight and accessibility.

Simon remembered being surprised at how quiet Gilbert was, considering how afraid of the dark he was. Clayton stared at his watch, counting each minute as it passed.

The boys looked back and forth from the closet panel to each other as they waited. Simon had thought he probably would have chosen the swim instead of being put in the closet.

One of the boys suggested Clayton let Gilbert out and Simon remembered him snapping and saying the ten minutes wasn't up yet. So, they waited in silence, surprised at the uneasiness of the quiet.

When Clayton's watch revealed that ten minutes had passed, Clayton slipped off the trim and pulled open the panel and Gilbert burst through the door screaming. He was panting and his face was red and hot. Through his sobs and bursts of hyperventilation, he yelled at his friends and asked them why they didn't let him out. Inside the room it must have been close to one hundred degrees and with no air, Gilbert was close to passing out.

The boys looked perplexed at Gilbert's rant and soon realized that the whole time he was locked in the closet he was screaming for help. Yet a few feet away none of the boys could hear him. Gilbert stormed down the steps of the deck and walked along the beach and dove into the water to cool off.

The boys were apologetic and had all felt bad that they stood nearby while their friend felt locked and near passing out. They each told Gilbert that there was no way they could hear him and if they had they would have opened the door. Gilbert forgave them before he went down to the beach for a swim, and as the other boys followed Gilbert for a late-night swim

Clayton was busying himself with the panel and returning the trim in place.

Clayton had not apologized to Gilbert and everyone was aware that he must have known that the small enclosure was soundproofed as well. When Simon had commented to Clayton that it was a bizarre closet to have, Clayton smiled and nodded. Then as he walked away Simon heard him say, 'You *could lock someone away for years and they would never find them.*'

"It was just creepy," Simon recalled. "It wasn't until later that we even asked each other why someone would need a room like that in the first place. I mean, his family was odd, but that is a whole other level of odd."

"You guys never told anyone?" Kerry asked.

"Who were we going to tell?" Simon said. "Plus, we were too young to know any better, I guess. We just made a pact to not speak about it ever again."

"And you think that Clayton would have taken Wayne there?" Kerry said.

"Well, if he had to get out of town quickly and get Wayne out of sight, there is no better place I guess."

The boat exited the channel and Simon turned left to where Clayton's cottage was situated. Kerry had never been to Clayton's cottage and could see how the cottagers out this far had greater privacy than the other cottages closer to town. As they approached the island Kerry could see the glow of light from inside the boathouse room. The yellow light radiated from the east-facing window and cascaded a path along the water toward the beach.

They spotted Clayton's boat tied to the finger dock that remained after all these years. Simon turned off the boat lights not wanting to be spotted by Clayton. He veered off to the right and cut the engine when they were near the shore and the Grew drifted the rest of the way in. Kerry grabbed the rope and jumped from the bow onto the cluster of rocks that ran most of the way along the shoreline. They secured the boat to a large jack pine that grew on an angle and hovered over the water's surface.

Together they walked quietly along the shore sticking to the shadows to prevent being seen.

From where they stood, they could see shadows move around the inside of the boathouse room, but they were unable to distinguish how many people were inside. They had thought reasonably that there were two but if working close to crime scenes taught Kerry anything it was to expect the unexpected.

They were standing underneath the raised boathouse and could hear the faint movement of steps coming from the room above them. Simon motioned with his fingers to the steps that led to the deck above.

Kerry was wondering what they were going to do when they got to the top when Simon suddenly pulled out a gun from the back of his waistband.

"Where did you get that?" Kerry asked.

"You know I have a hunting license," Simon whispered back.

"That," Kerry pointed. "Is not a hunting gun."

"No, but I also have been taking target practice over the last year," Simon said.

"Why?" Kerry asked.

"Can we talk about this later?" Simon asked.

Kerry nodded and began to follow Simon as he walked along the sand and began his climb up the wooden staircase to the boathouse deck. Peering through the railing as they neared the top, they could see the deck was clear and the door that led to the room on the boathouse was ajar.

Kerry could hear faint voices in conversation as they approached the opened door. She tried to look inside but could only glimpse the back of one man. He was standing next to a chair and was talking to someone on the other side of the room. She couldn't be certain if it was Clayton or not. She only saw him in his uniform and always in the light.

Simon pushed Kerry behind him and held his finger across his lips. He swung open the door just before he jumped into the room with his gun pointing at the person turned away from them.

"Don't move," Simon yelled.

Clayton pivoted on his feet and gasped at the sight of Simon holding a gun. While Simon held the gun on Clayton, Kerry could see a badly beaten Wayne slumped in the chair across the room. His arms were tied behind him and blood trickled down the front of his top. Clayton had removed the orange jumper that she last saw Wayne in, and he was dressed in a pair of grey sweats and a white t-shirt.

He still wore the prison-issued shoes without laces, and she couldn't tell if he was unconscious or if Clayton had already killed him.

"Wayne," Kerry shouted across the room, more of an instinct than a plan.

Wayne's head wobbled from side to side and a painful moan echoed from beneath his chin.

Clayton sprung toward Simon when he caught him looking over at Wayne and landed a punch on the side of his face. Simon fell backward and the gun tumbled from his hand, bouncing across the wood plank flooring and then came to rest under the sofa.

Clayton fell on top of Simon and wrapped his hands around Simon's neck and began to tighten his grip at the base of his throat.

Simon wrapped his hands around Clayton's wrists and pulled and fought to pry his fingers from their tight grasp. Kerry began to pound her fists on Clayton's back as she yelled for him to let go of Simon. In one swift movement, Clayton released his left hand and swung it around, and knocked Kerry sideways. She stumbled backward and hit the side of her head on the corner of the end table as she fell.

The dizziness was instantaneous when she collided with the wood. She watched through kaleidoscope vision as Simon and Clayton struggled on the floor. She could hear Wayne start to grow agitated behind her and the sound of his chair scratching the floor echoed as he wiggled around trying to loosen the ropes that secured him in place.

Kerry blinked away the blur in her vision as the two bodies twisted and rolled, and she could no longer tell which one was Simon and which one was Clayton. She squeezed her eyes together and yelled as she shook her head, and when she opened her eyes, she was able to see a little bit clearer. Her vision was still hazy, but she could distinguish Simon's patterned shirt from Clayton's plain black t-shirt.

Kerry grabbed hold of the table and raised herself up. She grabbed the lamp from the end table, raised it above her head, and brought it down with full force. The sound of hitting Clayton's skull with the weight of the lamp was more of a crunching sound than a crack.

Clayton's body slumped down and Simon pushed him off to the side where he rolled across the floor, landing face down and Kerry watched as blood began to trickle down the side of his face.

And Kerry was suddenly aware of the distinct scent of patchouli that filled the room.

32

Clayton was still unconscious when Simon and Wayne had lifted him onto a chair. Kerry crawled around on the floor swiping her arm under the sofa until she located Simon's gun. She pulled it out and held it by the handle. Wayne's wrists were raw from where Clayton tied his arms to the chair with old boat rope. The acrylic fiber ripped open Wayne's skin from where he struggled to free himself and blood dripped from the cuts. Kerry grabbed a towel from a hook on the wall and handed it to Wayne who began to dab at the wounds.

"How did you guys know to come here?" Wayne asked.

"It was Simon who guessed that Clayton may have brought you here," Kerry said.

"But how did you know Clayton was involved at all?" Wayne asked.

Kerry began to explain to Wayne about the note Jim was able to get to her before he died and how it led her to Clayton's sister where Lia's baby was found.

"I had called Peter to assist me once Simon realized we couldn't call Clayton. Simon convinced me to listen to your story once more, thinking that you were framed. When we realized Clayton took you from holding, we figured you were in danger. From there it was easy to see that Clayton was involved with Lia Bruce's death. We just don't know how or why," Kerry explained.

"I didn't know Jim had died," Wayne began to tear up. "Man, I have known him forever. He was one heck of a great guy."

"I agree," Kerry said. "The only thing I am confused about is how he could be involved with Lia's murder."

"Now that we have a name for our victim, does anyone know who she is?" Wayne asked.

"No, there are still so many holes in the story," Kerry said. "Jim's note was short. He wanted to let me know that Lia's baby had been taken and where he was, but he also wanted to let me know that although he didn't kill her, he felt guilty because he was wrapped up in the mess that got her in trouble. He apologized and asked me to forgive his deception, and begged me to not let his nephew and nieces think he had anything to do with the murder. No matter what, he wanted to make sure they didn't think he was a killer."

"I don't think anyone could ever think that of Jim," Simon said.

Kerry felt a pang of guilt as she stood near Simon and Wayne. The two men who trusted her and that she thought could have had something to do with the circumstances that led up to the murder of Lia Bruce.

"Did Jim give any clue to what Clayton was up to?" Wayne asked.

"He didn't even mention him in his note, he just insisted I take Simon and no one else. I guess he didn't think I would believe him if he told me Clayton was involved because he was a police officer."

"And the one person you were working closely with on the case," Wayne added.

Kerry reddened with embarrassment, "I am sorry Wayne."

Wayne waved off her apology, "Don't worry Kerry. The evidence did look pretty damning against me. I even started to believe the case against me."

"I had a hard time believing you had anything to do with the murder, or the fire, or even the explosion. I just never would have guessed it was Clayton who may have been the one behind it," Simon said.

"I get that he had access to all the information, what I don't understand is how and why Lia Bruce was murdered?" Kerry asked.

Clayton began to moan as he struggled into consciousness. The blood matted on the side of his hair and covered his ear. He raised his hand to his head when he realized what had happened. All three were standing in front of him, and Kerry handed the gun to Wayne who happily pointed it in Clayton's direction.

"Well, look who's awake," Wayne said.

"You three are a joke," Clayton mumbled through a half-laugh.

"We'll see about that when we get you back to town," Wayne said.

Clayton laughed, this time displaying blood-stained teeth in his mouth, "And what are you going to say?"

"That you dragged me out here to kill me," Wayne snapped.

"The way I remember it, you tried to escape from custody, and I managed to wrestle you down. I have a storeroom full of evidence that will prove you had reason to try and escape."

"There is only one problem with that Clayton," Kerry said.

"What is that?" Clayton said.

"Jim Chandler managed to get a note to me before he died," Kerry said, leaving the last sentence hanging in the air.

Clayton's smile dropped and he held Kerry's gaze with a steely glare.

"Do you want to know what Jim told me?" Kerry asked.

Clayton sat silent.

"He was feeling the weight of guilt over what happened to Lia Bruce and wanted to set some things straight for her baby," shock washed over Clayton's face and Kerry was aware she struck a chord.

"Yes, we know the victim's name is Lia Bruce," Kerry said. "What we don't know is why her son was with your sister?"

"You leave Patricia out of this," Clayton screamed. "She has no involvement in any of this!"

"It's not me you are going to need to convince. It's Constable George and the court that you are going to have to sway. You see Clayton, Patricia has been taken into custody this afternoon. She's going to be charged with Lia Bruce's murder as well as the kidnapping of her son. I figure that puts her at a ripe old age before she is free again," Kerry said.

Clayton lunged from the chair toward Kerry when Simon wielded his arm around and knocked him back into the chair, "Give me one more reason and I'll knock you into tomorrow."

Kerry smiled, "I am going to testify that we found Patricia completely ensconced with Lia Bruce's son in her home. And by the looks of things, she was setting up a permanent home for him. It's not going to look good Clayton. The sister of a police officer charged with murder and kidnapping."

Clayton looked from Wayne to Simon and then to Kerry, "What do you want from me? What will it take to leave Patricia out of this?"

"I can't say, Clayton. It's out of my hands," Kerry said.

"Everyone knows you have a bit of influence over Constable George. You can keep him off her if you want to," Clayton's tone begged Kerry for some sympathy. "Please."

"Why don't you start by telling me everything you know about what happened to Lia Bruce and how her son ended up in Patricia's care."

"There is more to this than you think. There are other people involved. Bad people. People that will stop at nothing to keep this information hidden," Clayton started to explain. "You have no idea how dangerous it can be if any of this gets out."

"Why don't you let us be the judge of that," Wayne said.

Clayton sighed and dropped his face into his hands before he began to speak.

"It began just after you got your break in court," Clayton said, looking directly at Wayne.

Wayne blushed, clearly uncomfortable with Kerry knowing the truth.

"When you had tried to get out of carrying those drugs from Warroad it scared a lot of guys who depended upon the steady stream of cash. You risked blowing it for everyone. That's why you were framed for the fire at Holmstrom's place."

Wayne's eyes widened, "You?"

Clayton nodded, "The guys you were dealing with came to me and offered me an opportunity to get in on the gig. They knew you had kept me out and they used it as an opportunity to get rid of you and keep their business running. It was easy to agree to. The money was easy, and I needed it if I was going to get out from underneath my drunk of a father, and support Patricia. She counted on me."

"But why not just let me out and you take my place?" Wayne asked.

"They didn't trust you to not go to the cops. They wanted to scare you," Clayton explained. "And it worked. You stayed quiet to protect your friends."

"Then what happened?" Wayne asked.

"I had to build up an operation, but it was getting harder with the increase in security at the border. Up until then, the waterway border was easy to travel through, but with the concern of illegal traffic, both countries beefed up their border security. The thing that is so funny, they were more worried about cigarettes and beer going across because of lost tax revenue. They had no idea that the operation had increased to hard drugs that were hitting the streets. It was an easy way to get them into the country, and once I got them into Lake Pines, I could get them on the trains and across the country within a few days."

"Who did you recruit?" Wayne asked.

"Do you remember Ellie? She had been dating Sam who got a part-time job at the train yard where his dad worked as a supervisor. Sam was happy to get the extra cash, and Ellie was easy to convince because she would do anything for Sam. Ellie would get the packages from me and then pass them onto Sam. Now, getting them across the border was getting harder and harder as time went on. That is where Jim came in. He was always the most mechanical out of all the kids I knew growing up. When I asked him to build a couple of underwater mini-subs, he had no idea what I wanted them for. He was just so excited to get paid to work on something he was passionate about. Once he had done a couple of jobs for me, he was officially involved. When he tried to get out, I threatened to let the guys in Warroad know and they would be happy to see both him and his business sink deep into the lake." Clayton gloated.

"You used Jim! He would never have been okay with running illegal drugs," Simon snapped, holding himself back from grabbing hold of Clayton's throat.

"He got over it soon enough when the money flooded in and he was able to buy that crappy marina for himself. All he had to do was keep the motors running and man the remote controls from his shop. He would drop them in the water and set them on a programmed course to our guys across the border. When they were filled, they would send a message to Jim and he would control the remote to return it to

Lake Pines. The border guards never knew what was happening right under their noses."

"You're a dirtbag, you know that?" Simon yelled.

"Yeah, well. Whatever," Clayton said. "We had a great system going. I had Jim working the logistics of getting stuff back and forth across the border. I had Ellie and Sam working the connections across the country and I had Bernard on hand to launder the money we were bringing in. It was a well-oiled machine." Clayton boasted.

"Then why become a cop?" Wayne asked. "I don't get it?"

"Because it was the perfect cover, that's why," Clayton explained.

Kerry ran through the names from Clayton's story. Ellie, Jim, Bernard. Ellie?

"Are you talking about Ellison Hanover?" Kerry asked.

Clayton nodded.

"So, the explosion?" Kerry asked.

"Yeah," Clayton said. "You were just a happy coincidence. I needed to get rid of the others because they wanted to disband our little deal when they found out about Lia."

"You killed them all?" Wayne asked. "And framed me."

"You have no idea how much money was coming in from this gig!" Clayton yelled.

"I have an idea after being at your place. The Lawren Harris hanging over your fireplace was suspiciously expensive for someone on a cop's salary." Kerry said.

Clayton nodded, "And that's not all of it either. There is a lot more if you let me go."

"Not a chance," Wayne snapped.

"How did Jesse Dale fit into all this?" Kerry asked, remembering the fourth victim from the explosion.

"He was one of the contacts in Warroad who was also trying to undermine our operation up here," Clayton said.

"And Lia?" Kerry finally asked. The reason she became involved in the mess that landed them here in Clayton's boathouse in Deception Bay.

A look of sadness covered Clayton's face. "I didn't want to kill her. I tried to convince her to change her mind."

"Change her mind about what?" Kerry asked.

"I met Lia when I was away at the academy. She was in nursing school and was working through one of her practicums at the academy. She was helping with checkups and things like that. Little stitches and injuries that needed mending were the perfect training for most of the nurses. I fell for her the second I saw her, and it was the same for her. We were inseparable the first year we dated. The second year we moved in together into a small apartment off-campus. It was my last year of training and she was going to finish her nursing degree a few months later.

"When I graduated ahead of her, I came to Lake Pines and started working at the police station and kept the businesses running with the others. I would go and visit Lia whenever I could, and I was eventually able to convince her to agree to move here. She was going to apply to the Lake Pines Hospital for a position on their nursing staff. It was when she was here for an interview with the hospital about a year ago when she first realized what I was doing. She had overheard me speaking with Jesse one time when he was in town and she figured out what we were doing. I was careless and I left some paperwork out on my desk at home. I usually locked it away, but I got sloppy. Anyhow, she high-tailed it out of here and back to her home when she realized what our operation was all about."

"How did she end up back in Lake Pines?" Kerry asked.

"She was back in town hoping to patch things up and to see if I would consider walking away from the smuggling. But I couldn't. It was too big for me to walk away from, and the operation was too massive for the guys in Warroad to let me go. That would have been fine, except she threatened to tell the police if I didn't walk away. She said it was for my own good. I agreed to her plan so that I could keep her quiet. Until I thought of a different option."

"And your plan was to kill her?" Kerry said.

"Not initially. I grabbed her on one of her runs and tried to scare her into not reporting me to the police. I pretended to be one of the guys from the U.S. and tried to scare her into staying quiet. But she had a bad history with drugs and didn't want to see other innocent kids hurt. She was addicted at a young age and it was difficult, but her family fought to get her clean. She enrolled in a nursing program and she graduated near the top of her class. Her life was back on track and she didn't want to be near anyone who had anything to do with drugs. Not even if she loved me." Clayton dropped his head and let out a sigh.

"So, you held her at Fox Lodge?" Kerry asked. "Why not here? In your crazy boathouse."

"She knew this place and I didn't want her to suspect I was the one who grabbed her. I really thought she would cave. Plus, in case I needed to pin anything on someone else I needed a location I had nothing to do with," Clayton coldly explained. "However, Lia wouldn't change her mind. No matter what I did she wouldn't break. She refused to change her mind. I tried for five days to convince her, and when it became evident she wasn't going to stay quiet, I had no choice but to kill her. It was the only way to keep her quiet." Clayton folded his hands over his face. "I loved her. You have to believe me."

As Clayton sobbed, the three stood shocked trying to absorb the story Clayton told them.

"And her baby?" Kerry asked, already knowing the answer to her own question.

"He's my son," Clayton said. Before he completely broke down in tears.

33

Noah was born without Clayton even knowing that Lia was pregnant. When she left Lake Pines after he refused to quit the smuggling operation, she had no idea she had become pregnant. She returned home to have her baby where her family could be close by and help her. It was where she felt safe. It was where she was able to straighten out her life. She called their son Noah because she felt like he was proof that there was promise after a tumultuous point in her life. She tried to put Clayton behind her and to move on, but the more she looked at Noah, the more she remembered how much she loved Clayton, and she returned to Lake Pines to try once more to get him to change his mind.

Lia thought that once he saw Noah and realized they had a child together, that he would see the importance of living a life away from the secret crime operation he built. They could have a good life together. Him working in the police station and her at the hospital.

The problem with Lia's plan wasn't Clayton but the men he worked for. The only way he was going to get out of his ties to the people in Warroad was if he was dead. If they found out about Noah, they would have surely used that to keep him pinned down too. He couldn't have that.

Clayton tried to change Lia's mind, he even tried to use her love for wanting to protect Noah against her. But in the end, it didn't work.

Lia died after being held in a cold dark stone shed for days when the man she loved plunged a knife deep into her heart. Her last thoughts before she died were of Noah and the smell of his hair when she kissed him goodnight.

Peter arrived at the cottage to arrest Clayton. After the statements were recorded and evidence sealed and bagged, Kerry climbed into the Grew with Wayne and Simon and headed back to town.

None of them knew where their lives would land next. Or what it would look like when they awoke the next morning.

34

It had been three days since Clayton was arrested. Wayne was cleared of all charges and was reinstated to his position in charge at the police station. His first day back on the job was spent organizing his files and revisiting his approach to details. He was committed to becoming a leader that Constable Peter George would be proud to have trained and he agreed to work closely with him over the next few months to reorganize his approach.

Simon, Kerry had learned, was secretly training with Wayne out at his cottage in preparation for writing his police examination entrance test. He wanted to surprise Kerry. He enjoyed his job at Fox Lodge as well as being a guide for tourists, but it wasn't going to be enough if he wanted to plan a life and a family with Kerry. Once Kerry knew about his plans to join the police force, he was able to explain how the mud on his boots matched the burial site on Tunnel Island. The night that Kerry went to search for the portable music device, Wayne brought Simon out to show him how to search a crime scene. It was Wayne who pointed his gun at Kerry thinking she was trespassing on the site. Once Wayne later found out it was Kerry, he stayed quiet not wanting to reveal Simon's secret. It also explained Simon's handgun and his proficiency in handling it. He had been going to a shooting range just outside of town to practice in preparation for his entrance test.

The day Kerry saw him in the diner with the young woman he was also working toward preparing for his test.

"I went to school with Barb. She is a member of the police force in Thunder Bay and she agreed to help me prepare for the written portion of the test that was coming up. It was an easy location to meet and she was going over some booklets she gave me to study from," Simon explained.

"I wish you would have come over and said something. I would have told you right then and there what I was doing," Simon paused. "I'm sorry you thought the worst of me."

"No, I'm sorry Simon," Kerry apologized. "I owe you and Wayne an apology. With just a few similarities to the evidence I had collected, I was willing to believe that you and Wayne could have been involved somehow."

"Clayton wanted you to believe those things Kerry," Simon consoled Kerry.

Simon also revealed that he had planned to propose the evening of the museum fundraiser. Then they had argued. He was so nervous at both the proposal and the upcoming police examinations that he blew everything out of proportion and just needed to get out of town for a bit. Then later when he found out she was thinking of accepting an offer to move back to Montreal and work with Jean, he put the idea of the proposal on hold.

Kerry didn't realize why Simon was so upset which set them further apart from each other. Simon had not wanted to sway her decision and he wanted her to make the choice that was right for her. It ended up forcing him to keep his plans to write the police examinations secret and led to her suspicions.

The council sorted out Bernard Wessex's mismanagement of funds and was able to pull off the museum renovation while keeping the city bank account in the black.

Jim's marina was sold to one of the young mechanics that was working for him and continued to operate under the same name.

Jim was laid to rest in Lake Pines' only cemetery which also boasted one of the best views of the lake. Most of the people from Lake Pines showed up for Jim's funeral and there were no shortages of stories sharing what a great friend Jim

Chandler was to each and every one of them.

Kerry decided to remember Jim exactly that way. Clayton took advantage of Jim and forced him into an illegal operation that he wouldn't have chosen to run if he was free to make that decision. In the end, Jim and the others could not stand by when they found out that Clayton had killed Lia when she threatened to reveal their operation.

They were planning to go to the court directly, bypassing the local police station for obvious reasons, and confess to the smuggling operation. They hoped that by offering information on Lia Bruce's murder that they would be given leniency on any other charges. The four were meeting at the coffee shop that morning in preparation for their afternoon meeting with the judge who had agreed to meet with them in private.

As it turned out, the judge who was unaware of Clayton's involvement had informed the police that he was to have a meeting with the four and it was about an international smuggling operation that was being run out of Lake Pines.

Once Clayton realized they were going to betray him, he tapped Jim's phone and found out they were meeting at the coffee shop in the morning. He quickly devised a plan to set the explosion so that it would not seem suspicious for all four to be killed at once.

He had even tried to convince Kerry to let someone else investigate because she was too close to the situation, but she refused.

Ultimately Jim's good conscience revealed Clayton's crime and before he died, he wanted to make sure that Lia Bruce found some justice and that her son, Noah, could be returned safely to her family.

With help from Peter's investigation team, Kerry was able to track down Lia Bruce's parents in Port Hope. Her parents were devastated at the news of Lia's murder but overwhelmed to learn that Noah was safe. Lia had never told them who Noah's father was, so they were never able to figure out to look in Lake Pines. Once Kerry revealed why Lia was reluctant to let Clayton into their lives, they understood.

When Lia's parents arrived in Lake Pines to get Noah, they told Kerry they wanted to see where Lia was found. It was important for them to know.

Kerry was hesitant, but after speaking with her parents in person she realized that the torment they had been through needed closure. And this was one step in attaining it. Kerry had Wayne and a team clean up the area as best as they could and remove any signs that it was a murder scene. Which meant removing the police tape and filling in the crime site as best they could.

The day Lia's parents arrived the warmth of spring had settled in every corner of Lake Pines. The air, even in the deep parts of the forest was warm and fragrant. Trees began to spring buds on their fragile branches and wildlife was beginning to appear with their babies. The grass had begun to green on the lawns and parks in town and everyone was eager to fill planters and gardens with bright flowers.

Kerry drove Lia's parents to Tunnel Island and was nervous as she led them to where Lia's body was found. Lia's mother carried Noah who shook a rattle and laughed, unaware of the sadness his grandparents were experiencing as they approached the spot their daughter was found.

Lia's parents stood for over half an hour looking out at the water from where their daughter was found.

"It's beautiful here," Lia's mother said. "We need to remember something beautiful out of all of this. Lia would want that."

Her father wrapped his arm around his wife and kissed the top of Noah's head.

Kerry watched as the family slowly began to heal. It was the first step in their obtaining closure to the saddest moment in their lives.

They planned to donate a bench that could be placed on the top of the hill that looked out into the water close to where Lia was found.

Fragrance wafted up where Kerry waited from a respectable distance from where the Bruce's stood. Lily of the Valley was blooming from the spring thaw and their miniature white bell-shaped flowers gave off a gentle perfume that filled the forest. Cedar, still damp from morning dew, gave a soothing undertone to the air. Kerry was astonished at how peaceful the spot could seem, even after knowing what happened here.

The following week a bench was delivered, purchased by Mr. and Mrs. Bruce, and was placed on the top of the hill looking out to the water.

On the back of the bench seat, a small brass plaque was affixed with an inscribed quote that Lia had used to keep her focus when she was working to get clean and start a new life. There was no name or date attributed to the quote.

It just simply read, "When I let go of what I am. I become what I might be."

35

Kerry had made her decision and telephoned Jean the moment she awoke. She realized she had to make the decision that was going to benefit her in the long term, and not just decide what was going to be best for 'right now'. Simon agreed to not pressure her while she was making her decision, giving her space and the time, she desperately needed.

Kerry knew that she couldn't put off telling Simon her decision and had planned to meet him for lunch later that day. They agreed to meet on the lawn of the museum. It looked out into the bay and gave them a clear view of the boats as they traveled in and out of Lake Pines. The breeze that blew up from the water, filled the air with the smell of the lake that only those that spent their life in Lake Pines could describe.

Simon was waiting for Kerry on a blanket he spread out under a large oak tree. He had packed her favorite lunch and grabbed two hot coffees from the restaurant across the street. Kerry's heart warmed as she saw Simon waiting for her.

She sat beside him and leaned in to kiss him. Kerry dragged her teeth across her lower lip and blushed as Simon looked into her eyes. She didn't like small talk when she was nervous and was never good at hiding her feelings when something was bothering her. She placed the coffee on a flat surface of the ground next to her and then turned to Simon.

"I've made a decision with regards to Montreal," Kerry began.

Simon's body tensed and he sat still as she spoke.

"I called Jean this morning. He's been very patient waiting for my answer. He knew I just wanted to wait until the investigation was over. It's been a month now and I have thought a lot about it. If I go to Montreal, I'll have more interesting cases to work on and more funding to back me up."

"Yes, you will," Simon agreed.

"And I also have been offered a position teaching at the university once a week, which I have always wanted to do."

"Uh-huh," Simon nodded.

"The problem is, I am not ready to leave," Kerry said.

"Lake Pines?" Simon asked.

"You," Kerry answered, setting all of Simon's concern at ease.

Simon wrapped his arms around Kerry and held her tight. "That's good. Because I am not ready to lose you."

Simon was relieved. He also had news to share. He had been accepted into a program that is being spearheaded by Constable George that would allow him to be trained while working out of Lake Pines as a junior officer.

They sat together making plans for their future which now seemed within their grasp. But whatever they do, and whatever happens to them along the way, their lives will be together here in Lake Pines.

* * *

Wayne came barreling down the hill with his arms flailing at his side as he was yelling Kerry's name.

Kerry and Simon turned around just as Wayne stopped short behind them, almost falling into their lunch. He leaned forward, resting his hands on his knees, and dropped his head down as he tried to catch his breath.

"What is wrong Wayne," Kerry asked.

"A body has been found at Ascot Cottage," Wayne wheezed.

"Then call the police," Kerry said, trying not to laugh.

"I need you to come out there with me," Wayne said.

"Why? Do you suspect foul play?" Kerry asked.

"I think so. The maintenance man discovered the body," Wayne explained. "And there's evidence he was poisoned. And there is more, but I will tell you on the way."

Wayne walked past them both, and to the dock at the marina where his boat was moored.

For Simon and Kerry, the time for a long lunch had passed, as too did their talk of planning a future.

At least for the moment.

All that was left for the rest of the day was to find a murderer.

THE END

Author's Note

Thank you for reading, and I sincerely hope you enjoyed Death At Deception Bay, the second book in the Lake Pines Mystery Series.

Please check out the other books in the Lake Pines Mystery Series.

For a chance to win a free book, sign up at:

www.llabbott.com/book-giveaway

Every month there's a new contest and every name on my email list is entered to win. Over and over and over again. Plus, you'll be the first to know about new releases or sales. Your personal information will never be divulged, shared, or sold.

If you're on social media. . . I would love to have you follow along.

Thanks again, my best to you and yours.
L.L. Abbott

Books by L.L. Abbott

Mystery & Suspense

Thrillers

Teen & Young Adult

General Fiction

372

Manufactured by Amazon.ca
Bolton, ON